The Lost Clue

by
Mrs. O. F. Walton

The Lost Clue
by Mrs. O. F. Walton

Copyright © 2024

All Rights reserved.

No part of this publication may be reproduced, stored in a retrieval system, or transmitted in any form or by any means, electronic, mechanical, photocopying or Otherwise, without the written permission of the publisher.
The author/editor asserts the moral right to be identified as the author/editor of this work.

ISBN: 978-93-64283-67-0

Published by

DOUBLE 9 BOOKS

2/13-B, Ansari Road
Daryaganj, New Delhi – 110002
info@double9books.com
www.double9books.com
Tel. 011-40042856

This book is under public domain

ABOUT THE AUTHOR

Mrs. O. F. Walton, was an English author of Christian children's books, primarily but not solely fiction. She was the daughter of an Anglican clergyman and married his curate, with whom she spent four years in Jerusalem. Amy was the daughter of John Deck (1815-1882), the vicar of St Stephen's Church on Spring Street in Hull, and Mary Ann Sanderson Gibson (1813-1903), a hymnist. Her writings began with My Mates and I, which was written in 1870 but not published until 1873. Meanwhile, her first published work, My Little Corner, appeared in 1872. Christie's Old Organ, one of her most famous books, was published in 1874 and has been reproduced on a regular basis until today. The book was imported to Japan in 1882 and published in 1885 in a translation by Tajima Kashi, making it one of Japan's first publications on the history of Christian and children's literature. It was translated twice more: in 1903 and in 1994. In 1875, Amy married Octavius Frank Walton, her father's curate at the time. Mrs. O. F. Walton, her husband's name, is how she became more well-known. They relocated to Jerusalem the same year they married, and Octavius served in a church on Mount Zion until 1879. Meanwhile, her novel A Peep Behind the Scenes was released there in 1877.

CONTENTS

CHAPTER I
IN THE ARCADE 7

CHAPTER II
A DIFFICULT POSITION 12

CHAPTER III
CAPTAIN FORTESCUE'S PROMISE 18

CHAPTER IV
A TROUBLED NIGHT 25

CHAPTER V
THE SAFE OPENED 29

CHAPTER VI
THE TWO ENVELOPES 36

CHAPTER VII
A WALK THROUGH BORROWDALE 45

CHAPTER VIII
HONISTER CRAG 55

CHAPTER IX
A FINISHED CHAPTER 64

CHAPTER X
GOOD-BYE 71

CHAPTER XI
DAISY BANK 76

CHAPTER XII
BLACK COUNTRY ROSES 85

CHAPTER XIII
MOTHER HOTCHKISS 90

CHAPTER XIV
THE OLD OAK CUPBOARD 97

CHAPTER XV
  156, LIME STREET 105

CHAPTER XVI
  THE BLOTTED WORD 110

CHAPTER XVII
  A STRANGE LETTER 116

CHAPTER XVIII
  WORDS TO BE REMEMBERED 122

CHAPTER XIX
  GRANTLEY CASTLE 125

CHAPTER XX
  THE PHOTO OF A FRIEND 132

CHAPTER XXI
  LORD KENMORE 140

CHAPTER XXII
  MR. NORTHCOURT'S OPINION 146

CHAPTER XXIII
  A MOST CHARMING GIRL 151

CHAPTER XXIV
  THE PICTURE GALLERY 156

CHAPTER XXV
  WAITING FOR THE ANSWER 163

CHAPTER XXVI
  A CHRISTMAS JOURNEY 169

CHAPTER XXVII
  ANOTHER CHAPTER CLOSED 178

CHAPTER XXVIII
  WATENDLATH FORGET-ME-NOT 183

CHAPTER XXIX
  THE MISSING WORD FOUND 189

CHAPTER I
IN THE ARCADE

NEW Street Station, Birmingham, is an exceedingly busy place at all times of the day; but at certain hours, when many trains are due, the bustle, hurry, and rush, in every part of it, are beyond description. Two great lines, the London and North-Western and the Midland, run through it; and although, to the initiated, there is nothing more easy than to locate the part of the station in which the various trains will arrive or from which they will depart, yet to a stranger in Birmingham, especially to one who has come from the quiet of some remote country place, the six different platforms, the numerous booking offices, and the busy stream of human life crossing and re-crossing the great bridge which spans the station from side to side, are both bewildering and perplexing.

It was at the busiest time of the ever-busy New Street day, that the London express came thundering into the station. It had rushed on like some great monster of the deep, flying through air instead of water, puffing, snorting, panting, but never once stopping after leaving Euston, until it came running triumphantly into Birmingham, having accomplished its journey of over a hundred and twelve miles in the short space of two hours.

As it steamed in, a long line of expectant porters awaited its arrival, and, as it began to slacken its speed, they kept their eyes fixed on the line of first-class carriages, for that way lay "tips." There was a dining-saloon on the train, and the first-class part of it was well filled. Most of the passengers were, however, going on further; but one gentleman, with a long kit-bag in his hand, came to the carriage door and prepared to alight from the train.

The porters made a rush in his direction, all eager to relieve him from his burden, and thereby to secure the bakhshish which English porters, as well as Arab ones, are seldom backward in scenting from afar.

The gentleman selected one of the group and handed him the bag, whilst the others retired discomforted.

"Where for, sir?"

"The Midland train north. Which platform will it be?"

"Number 5, sir. Any luggage in the van?"

"No, none. Let me see; it starts at 5.30. An hour to wait, I believe."

"Not quite, sir; you're late a bit. It isn't often the express loses a minute, but she's five minutes late to-day."

The traveller took out his watch to compare it with the great station-clock, and then followed the porter up the steps to the bridge. Arrived at No. 5, he dismissed the man, who departed with a beaming countenance, as he pocketed double the sum which he had expected to receive.

For some minutes the young man, for he was not more than twenty-five, paced the platform restlessly. He was impatient of the delay, and the noise and racket of the station jarred upon his nerves. The shriek of an approaching train, the rattle of a departing one, the rumble of the porters' trucks, the shouting of the newspaper boys, the ceaseless rush of people in all directions, tired him that day, he hardly knew why. He had not come from the country, and he was accustomed to London streets and London stations; he did not mind noise at other times, but to-day he felt as if he could not stand the discordant sounds for another hour. He resolved to leave the station, and to take a walk in the city until it was time for his train.

He left his bag at the Midland Luggage Office, climbed the long flight of steps in the midst of a continuous stream of people, passed with them a similar stream pouring downwards into the station, and then made his way to the street beyond.

As he did so, more than one person turned to look at him. He was a man who, even in a crowd, attracted attention. Tall and well built, he was every inch a soldier; his profession was patent to all who saw him; but it was not that which caused the passers-by to notice him, and to look after him as he walked on. It was not so much his upright manly figure, as his extremely handsome face, with its refined features, which made him a marked man. His dark hair, hazel eyes, long eyelashes, aquiline nose, and short upper lip, gave him a decidedly aristocratic appearance, which could not fail to strike the most casual observer.

"One of the upper ten, I should say!" remarked one man to another, as he crossed the station yard and turned into Corporation Street.

The shop windows were all lighted up, for it was December, and quite dark at half-past four. The street was crowded, for it was close upon Christmas, and multitudes of people, men, women, and children, were doing their Christmas shopping, or gazing idly into the brilliantly illuminated windows. But in spite of the crowds, he was glad he had come, for there were none of the discordant sounds of the station, and the keen air was refreshing to him after its close atmosphere.

A row of flower-sellers stood in the road at the edge of the pavement, and he stopped to buy a bunch of violets from a girl who looked tired and cold. He did not want the violets, but he was touched by her face, and he gave her three times the price that she asked for them.

Then he turned into the Arcade, which was a blaze of electric light. All the shops were displaying choice and attractive articles suitable for Christmas presents. In a niche in the wall, near one of the toy-shops, there stood on a pedestal an old man. He was dressed in red cloth, trimmed with swansdown, with long white hair and beard, and with a cocked hat on his head. He was supposed to represent Father Christmas, and he, too, looked cold and tired as he stood, motionless as a waxwork figure, taking no notice of the busy scene around him. A group of children had gathered at the foot of the pedestal, and were looking up in his face with admiring glances, hoping to beguile him to fill their stockings on Christmas Eve with all the pretty things their hearts desired.

On the right hand side of the Arcade were several jewellers' shops, a glittering mass of beauty. Tiny electric lamps illuminated the countless sparkling and costly articles exposed for sale, and made them even more bewitching and tempting than they had appeared by daylight. The door of one of these shops opened just as he passed it, and a young lady, stylishly dressed, and wearing beautiful ermine furs, came out of it. She caught sight of him immediately, and put out her hand as she exclaimed, in a surprised voice—

"Captain Fortescue! You here?"

"Yes, Lady Violet, and I never dreamt of seeing you. What are you doing in Birmingham?"

"We're staying with the De Courcys, only six miles out, and we've come in to do a little Christmas shopping, as we shan't have much time after we get home. Isn't it strange we should meet? Why, we haven't seen you since that jolly time in the Riviera! Come and speak to mother; she is in this shop buying Maude a bracelet. She promised her one for Christmas, and she thought Maude had better choose it herself; but she can't make up her mind, and I was coming outside to look at one we saw in the window. Come in, and give us your advice."

Captain Fortescue followed her into the jeweller's and saw the two ladies standing at the counter and bending over it. It was covered with bracelets of every variety, all of them sparkling with jewels and exceedingly beautiful and costly.

"Mother, whom do you think I found in the Arcade? Look here!"

The elder lady turned round. "Captain Fortescue! Is it possible? I'm delighted to see you again; we haven't seen you for months. Where are you stationed now?"

"I'm at Aldershot at present, but we're likely to be moved soon. I wrote to Evelyn, but he hasn't answered my letter."

"Naughty boy! He's a shockingly bad letter writer; he always was. But what are you doing in Birmingham?"

"I'm only passing through," said the Captain, looking at his watch. "I'm going on by the five-thirty, Lady Earlswood."

"How lucky we just met you! Now you must come and see us soon. We're having a large house-party for Christmas. Can't you join us? Evelyn will be at home."

"Yes, do come," said Lady Violet. "It will be like having those dear old days in the Riviera back again, and I want you to see the photos I took then. They have come out splendidly."

"I should like to come very much, but I'm afraid it is impossible."

"Is it really quite impossible?" said Lady Earlswood. "Do try to arrange it."

"I'm afraid I shall not be able to do so. You see, my poor old father has not been very well lately—in fact, I am going there now. What is the matter I don't quite know yet. I had a letter from him yesterday morning, written apparently in good spirits, and then to-day I had a wire begging me to go at once. If he is ill and needs me, of course whatever leave I get, I must spend with him."

"Yes, of course; but it may not be that. He may want to see you for some other reason. If so, do let me know. Just send me a line or a wire with the one word 'Coming.' That will be quite enough."

"Thank you, Lady Earlswood, I shall certainly not forget. Now I must leave Lady Maude to choose her bracelet and hurry back to New Street."

"Must you really? Can't you have tea with us at Fletcher's? We are going there in a minute or two."

"I'm afraid not. I shall miss my train if I do."

He said good-bye to them, and walked quickly down the Arcade, but Lady Violet came to the door again to look at another bracelet in the window—at least, so she said; but her eyes, when she got outside, were certainly not turned in the direction of the brightly-lighted shop window.

"How little they know," he said to himself, as he went down the crowded steps to Platform No. 5. "I sometimes think I ought to tell them that I am not one of themselves."

CHAPTER II
A DIFFICULT POSITION

CAPTAIN FORTESCUE was in good time for his train, and secured a corner seat in the carriage. He bought a book at the stall and opened it when the train started, but he read only a few pages. He was wondering why his father had sent for him, and what explanation of the telegram he would receive on his arrival.

When he was last at home, he had thought his father was aged and altered, and therefore he had suspected that illness was the reason of his summons. Yet, from the letter received the day before, he had evidently been out as usual, and it contained no hint of his feeling indisposed at the time of writing it. Was there any other cause which had led to this unexpected and sudden call to return home at once?

Between Captain Fortescue and his father there was nothing whatever in common. Their ideas, their way of looking at things, their habits of life were totally and diametrically opposed. His father was a wealthy man, but not even his son could stretch his filial affection sufficiently far to call him a gentleman.

Mr. Fortescue was a man who had risen, people were accustomed to say, when they spoke of him. And yet he had not risen. His position in life was altered; instead of being a miner, obliged to work hard for his daily bread, he had become a landed proprietor. How this had been accomplished, his son had not the remotest idea; but he had never risen. He was exactly the same uneducated, vulgar man that he had been in his days of hard work and poverty. He could barely read or write, both were done in his own fashion, and he never made the slightest effort to improve in either. He cared for little but eating and drinking: he domineered over his servants and dependants at one moment, and spoilt them the next: he was lavish in his expenditure at times, and at other times would haggle over a halfpenny: he had not even learnt to speak King's English; his talk was the talk of the mine; even his groom could speak more grammatically, and could express himself with a less provincial accent.

No one realized all this more than Mr. Fortescue's own son; and yet it gave him a pang even to harbour the thought of it for a moment. For he had been a good father to him in many ways. He had shouted at him and blustered at him from his youth up, but he had never grudged him anything. He had lavished money in the most prodigal way on his son's education. He had sent him to the most expensive preparatory school that could be found, when he was only seven years old. From thence, the boy had gone to Eton, and in due course had passed into Sandhurst. No nobleman's son had ever had more spent upon him. The best coaching that London could produce had been his; he had been given every opportunity, every possible advantage.

Fortescue had been gazetted to a cavalry regiment, and his pay consequently was far from adequate for his expenses; but no money that he needed was withheld from him. A handsome allowance was supplemented by numerous cheques, to supply the wherewithal for various outgoings in the way of travelling or pleasure. The Honourable Evelyn Berington, Lady Earlswood's younger son, who had been his friend throughout the whole of his Sandhurst course, had far less money to spend than he had. And all this made Fortescue feel that, whatever his father might be, and however much his lack of refinement might jar upon him, it was his bounden duty to give him the affection and respect due from a loyal and grateful son. Besides which, Kenneth Fortescue was a man of honest religious belief. He knew the requirements of the Fifth Commandment. He know that, so far as it was possible for him to honour his father, that honour must be readily and cheerfully given.

And yet, at times, the incongruity of his position was keenly realized by him. He felt it very strongly on this particular December night, when he was being carried away swiftly into the darkness north of Birmingham. That was the real reason which prevented him from reading as he journeyed on; he was too busy doing battle with himself; he was fighting against his natural repugnance to all that was common or vulgar, his innate shrinking from the home where refinement of feeling or expression found no place. He was deeply grateful to his father for all that he had done for him in the past; and yet, that night, he was inclined to think that it had been a terrible mistake. He had been educated out of his proper position; his friends and acquaintances were all men moving in an utterly different circle; his sympathies and interests and attractions were in a sphere which he could never have any right to enter. If Lady Earlswood had seen his father, she would never have dreamt for a moment of inviting him to her Christmas house-party or of reckoning him amongst her friends.

Captain Fortescue was a most honourable man, and he felt sometimes as if he were a walking impostor. There had been times when he had suddenly felt it incumbent on him to tell them the truth, and had even been on the very verge of doing so. As they had walked together by the sea, under the blue Italian sky, he had, more than once, been on the point of blurting out the fact that he was the son of a man who had once been a common miner.

He had, however, at the last moment, withheld from making this disclosure; not so much because he was afraid of what they might think of him, or of how they might treat him, but because he had felt that it would be hardly treating his father fairly, were he to reveal what that father had told him in the strictest confidence. If he, by his honest toil, had earned the money to place himself in a position of affluence, and moreover to give his son the education of a gentleman, was it right that that son should publish his father's humble origin to the world?

Thus time had drifted on, and he had moved in the highest circles, and had been received into the best society, and no one knew anything of his father beyond the fact that he lived at Ashcliffe Towers, near Sheffield, had a large estate, and was evidently a very wealthy man.

When, two hours later, the train ran into the large Sheffield station, his thoughts were still pursuing the same unpleasant and difficult course. He called a hansom and was soon driving rapidly through the busy streets and out towards the country beyond. As he went, he wondered again what he should find at his journey's end, and whether his father would come out as usual to welcome him on his arrival. After about half an hour's drive, the cab turned in at a lodge gate, and he could see, through the fir trees in the avenue, the lights in the windows of his home.

An old butler came to the door in answer to the cabman's ring. He had lived with his father for years, and had known him from a boy. Mr. Fortescue objected to keeping many servants; they were only a trouble, he said, and he did not care to have a young jackanapes of a footman to stand and watch him when he ate. Elkington had white hair, and his hand trembled as he took the bag from the driver. He did not speak until the man had driven off, and then he said:

"I'm glad you've come, sir!"

"What's the matter, Elkington? Is my father ill?"

"Very ill, sir," said the old man. "Come into the library, sir; the doctor's upstairs now."

"That bag's too heavy for you, Elkington! It makes you pant: let me take it."

"No, no, sir; I can manage all right. I'm getting a bit short of wind, that's all."

"I heard from my father yesterday; he seemed quite well then."

"Yes, sir; and he was all right yesterday, and when he got up this morning. He came down to breakfast as usual; he always will have it at eight, you know. Well, he'd just sat down and was beginning, when there come a big ring at the front door bell. It's Watson's duty to go to the door when I'm waiting, but she never came down, and just as I was getting the master his bacon, the bell rings again. Well, he shouted and he stormed—beg your pardon, sir; you know how he carries on; you'll forgive me saying it."

"I know, Elkington; go on."

"So I put the bacon down, sir, and I went myself to see who was there. It was a boy with a telegram; he held out the yellow envelope to me, and he stood waiting while I took it in to the master.

"'What have you got there, Elkington?' he said. And when he saw what it was, he turned the colour of the table-cloth—that ghastly and white.

"'Take it out of the envelope, Elkington,' he says, 'my hand trembles so.'

"So I took it out and handed it to him, and he just looked at it one minute, and then he fell back in his chair in a dead faint, and the telegram slipped down on the floor under the table. I was that frightened, sir, I didn't know what to do. And then Watson came running in to know what was the matter. She do give herself airs, that woman, sir! Well, if you'll believe me, she swept me aside, and she took the master in her charge, and no one should touch him or do anything for him but herself. I said I would go for the doctor, and she said, 'No, I shouldn't, and he would be all right presently.'

"By-and-by the telegraph boy comes out of the hall and asks, 'Is he wanted, and is there any answer?' So I went out and sent him off; and I ran in the front and told Roger, the garden-boy, to fly off for Dr. Cholmondeley. Even Watson was glad when he came, for we thought he was dead, but the doctor brought him round; it was weakness of the heart, he said, and he was to be kept very quiet."

"I'm glad you sent for me, Elkington."

"It was the master did that, sir. I went in his room to take some hot water, and I heard him say to Watson: 'Send for the Captain,' he says. 'No, sir, you keep quiet,' she says; 'you don't want the Captain here; you're all right now.' You'd never believe, sir, how that woman lords it over him!

Why, none of the rest of us dares to contradict the old gentleman; but, ever since she came here, she's been worming herself into his favour, and making herself that useful to him he thinks he can't get on without her. But this time she was not going to get her own way. I heard what she said, and I went up to the bed and said: 'Shall I wire for the Captain, sir?' and the old gentleman nodded his head, and Watson looked as if she would kill me. She doesn't like you, doesn't Watson, sir."

"I know she doesn't, and I don't like her."

"So I sent off the wire, and I'm glad you've come, sir; you weren't long getting off."

"No, Elkington, but I only just caught the express. Is that the doctor coming down?"

"I believe so, sir; I'll bring him in here."

The next minute the doctor entered. He was a middle-aged man, with a quiet, dignified manner which inspired confidence in his patients.

"Captain Fortescue, I believe."

"Yes, doctor; I am very anxious to hear what you think of my father."

"It's a case of shock," said the doctor. "He received some bad news, I gather, this morning, and that is a great strain upon a man of his age. The action of the heart is weak—in fact, it had nearly ceased altogether. He has pulled round a little now, but there may be a relapse at any time."

"Perhaps I had better not see him to-night."

"Under ordinary circumstances I should most certainly have agreed with you, but he is most anxious to see you. He heard the cab stop, and he asked if you had come. Watson advised him to wait a little. Good faithful soul that Watson, I should imagine!"

Captain Fortescue did not answer.

"You don't like her?"

"No, I don't, but I really can hardly tell you why. Then you think I had better go up?"

"Yes, if he insists upon seeing you. Did it ever occur to you that he might have some special reason for wishing to see you, something that he wanted particularly to say to you or to ask you?"

"No. Has he, do you think?"

"I fancy so. I may be wrong, mind you, but I've a great idea that it is something more than mere affection that has made him so anxious for you to arrive. I have been in several times to-day, and each time he has asked if the Captain has come, and whether I thought he would be able to speak to the Captain when he did come."

"Well, I shall see when I go up," said Captain Fortescue. "I don't know in the least what it could be."

A knock at the door interrupted them.

"Come in," said the Captain.

A middle-aged woman entered. She was short in stature, with sharp features and a receding chin, and was heavily marked by smallpox.

"Has my father sent for me, Watson?"

"No, sir, he does not feel well enough to see you now; he will see you after dinner."

With these words, she left the room.

"Better so," said the doctor, as he took leave; "better for you and better for him."

CHAPTER III
CAPTAIN FORTESCUE'S PROMISE

WHEN Dr. Cholmondeley had gone, and whilst the old butler was laying the cloth in the dining-room, the Captain sat in an armchair by the fire in the library. How well he knew that room, and how the handsome vulgarity of its furniture had appalled him in days gone by! The gaudy amber-coloured carpet with its huge floral pattern; the table-cloth of velvet plush, but of a different red from that of the carpet; the massive bookcase with its rows of books, chosen because of their gilded binding, but in total disregard of their contents; the pictures on the walls, selected for the splendour of their frames, but possessing nothing in themselves to charm the artistic eye; the great mirror in its elaborate gilt setting; the massive coal-box with its startling pictorial design; the bright blue curtains in the window embellished with a golden pattern; the very ornaments standing on the mantleshelf,—one and all, were costly and magnificent indeed, but at the same time utterly lacking in the very elements of taste or beauty. These, however, he passed over to-day, without even bestowing upon them a single sigh of regret, as he thought of the large sums of money which had been wasted upon them.

But one object in the room he did look at and sigh over, and that was a large picture, hung in a gorgeous gilt frame on the wall, just opposite the chair in which he was sitting. It was the full-length portrait of a woman of about forty, with dark hair, high cheek-bones, and a very red face. She was arrayed in gaudy colours, which harmonized as little with each other as did the colours of the room. It was a heavy, stupid face, with hardly a gleam of intelligence in it.

Captain Fortescue gazed at it, and a pained expression came into his face as he did so. It was the picture of his mother! He had never seen his mother; she had died when he was a few months old, and he often wished that he had never seen her picture. He could have drawn her so differently with the pen of imagination. He could have painted her in such subdued and beautiful colours. He would have made her tall and fair and lovely, with a sweet, gentle face, a graceful figure, and with eyes which had a world of tenderness in them. But here was her picture drawn from life, and she was his mother, and he must try to think as dutifully of her as he could.

Again he said to himself that his father's generosity to him had been a mistake; it had caused him to have feelings and ideals out of keeping with his position; it had made him even dissatisfied with his own mother.

"Dinner is ready, sir," said Elkington's voice behind him.

"Elkington."

"Yes, sir."

"What became of that telegram?"

"It's here, sir, somewhere on the writing-table; I put it there myself. Oh, here it is under this letter-weight. I'm afraid it's bad news, sir; you'll excuse my having read it, but it was lying open on the floor."

Captain Fortescue took the pink paper, opened it, and held it to the light.

It contained these words:

"Mine flooded—all lost—utter ruin."

"What does that mean, Elkington? My father never told me any of his business affairs. Had he money in a mining company?"

"I believe so, sir; I'm afraid so. I think he must have lost heavily, and I think, too, he must have feared bad news this morning, he turned so white when I brought the telegram in."

The Captain did not eat much dinner, and was glad when the last course had been cleared away. "Now, Elkington, see if I can go to my father."

The old man soon returned with the message that his master would like to see the Captain at once. He therefore went up the wide staircase, and crossed the landing to his father's room. The door was open, and he could see Watson standing by the bed and giving him something from an invalid cup.

"Father, I'm sorry to find you in bed," he said, as he went forward.

"Yes, Ken, I've had a bad turn this time. I'm glad you've come. Watson, you can go and get your supper; do you hear? And don't come till I ring for you."

Watson put down the cup with a bang, as if she resented being dismissed, and stalked out of the room.

"Has she gone, Ken?"

"Yes, father."

"See if she's shut the door."

No, the door was ajar, but the Captain closed it, and turned the key in the lock.

"I'm very ill, my boy."

"Dr. Cholmondeley hopes you may feel better soon; I've been talking to him downstairs."

"Look 'ere, Ken, I don't believe in doctors; they say what they think folks will like. I know better."

"Don't tire yourself, father."

"I must tire myself, Ken; I've got something as I want to say to you. I'm not a-going to put it off, or it may be too late. I got a telegram to-day."

"Yes, I saw it downstairs. What does it mean?"

"It means I'm ruined, Ken; that's what it means!"

"How ruined? In what way?"

"Why, all my money was in that there mine, every farthing of it!"

"Surely not all!"

"It was, Ken; they paid five, ten and twelve per cent. sometimes, but it was all a humbugging affair, as it turns out. I got a letter only yesterday from a man as I know, who has shares in it, too, and he told me as how he was a-going to sell out, and I meant to do the same. I should have done it to-day; but it's too late now; that there wire was from him."

"How terrible!" said the Captain.

"Terrible! I should just think it is, Ken; and all your money was there, too."

"My money?"

"Well, yes; money as I had to spend for you; but it's gone along of the rest. I've given you a good eddication, Ken; no one can say as I haven't. I've not stinted you, have I?"

"Never, father, never."

"I've done my best for you, ever since you was a little lad—a little motherless lad, Ken."

"You have, father, you have."

"And if this mine hadn't gone smash, I should have left you a rich man."

"Never mind about me, father; I'm very sorry for you."

"Well, I'm not long for this world, Ken, so it matters little for me; but I'm glad you've come. I wanted to see you and put matters straight for you. When I'm gone—"

"Don't talk like that, dad—" his old name for his father in his boyish days—"I hope you'll soon be much better."

"Perhaps so, Ken, but perhaps not. Now, listen! When I'm gone, you take this 'ere key, you see it on this bunch, it's the one with a bit of pink string tied round it."

"What key is it?"

"It's the key of the safe over there, in the corner of my room, just by the cupboard door there. Open the safe, and you'll see my will; it's not worth the paper it's written on now. Well, underneath the will you'll see an envelope addressed to you."

"To me, father?"

"Yes, Ken; you take that there envelope, and inside of it you'll find some information as you ought to have. Follow it up, Ken, and I hope as it will put you all right."

"What is it about, father? Let me get the paper now."

"No, no; I won't have it opened till I'm gone; time enough then—time enough then."

"Shall I take the key?"

"No, no; leave it on the table beside me. I'll have no one meddling with my keys whilst I'm here to look after them. Put the bunch where I can see it as I lie here. Get me a drink, Ken. I feel a bit faint."

Captain Fortescue held the cup to his lips.

"There, there, that's better, lad; raise me a little."

"Won't you be quiet now, father? You've talked enough; let me call Watson."

"No, no; I haven't told you yet what I want to say. Who's that at the door?"

There was a low knock.

It was Watson.

"The master mustn't talk any more," she said. "Dr. Cholmondeley would be very much displeased."

"You mind your own business," said her master.

"Let me give you some milk, sir."

"I've had some. Go away, Watson; I want to speak to my son. Don't you come till I send for you!"

Watson bounced out of the room and slammed the door after her, and once more father and son were left alone.

"Ken, keep that woman out till I've told you what I want to tell you. Is the door shut?"

"Quite shut, father."

"Well, you remember a man of the name of Douglas?"

"No, I don't."

"Oh no, of course you don't. He was parson of the church here when you were away at boarding school; he was only here a few months. I was churchwarden then, and so I saw a good bit of the parson. Well, he preached one Sunday in the church, and the next day I heard as how he was dying. He'd broke a blood-vessel or something o' that sort. He sent across to know, would I go and see him, and when I gets there he says to me:

"'Now, Fortescue,' he says, 'you've handled a lot o' money in your day, and you know what to do with it, and I want you to be so good as to help my wife when I'm gone.' She were there, sobbing away by his bed, a fine-looking woman too! 'I haven't much to leave her and the children,' he says. 'She has a little bit o' money of her own, but all as I've saved I've paid away for insurance, in case anything should happen to me. Now, what I want you to do,' he says, 'is this: to help her to get that money invested in something as will bring her in a good interest, and yet be a safe concern. Now I've never had much to do with money,' he says, 'I've had so little of it; but you've made a big pile, and you do know, and so I want you to help the wife when I'm gone.'

"Well, I promised him, Ken, and that night the poor fellow died. She got her insurance money, and I took charge of it for her and said as how I would invest it and send her the interest. I put it into India three and a half per cents., and forwarded her the dividends reg'lar, just as they came to me. Then this gold mine in Brazil was started, and I put all my own money in it, and I got rattling good returns, and thinks I, why shouldn't poor Mrs. Douglas have a slice of good luck along of me?

"So I put her money in it too. I ought to have asked her leave, Ken, but I didn't. You see, we'd had a bit of a tiff just at that time. She lived in York then, and I used often to run over when her interest was due and take it with me instead of writing; it seemed friendly-like. And I took a great fancy to her, and I wanted her to come and be your ma; but she wouldn't hear of it, and drew herself up, and looked at me in such a way it fair scared me. So I didn't want to go and see her, and I'm a bad hand at letters. I just sent her the money and said I was glad the interest was better, and Ken, she believes to-day that it's still in the India three and a half per cents.!"

"Do you mean to say, father, that all Mrs. Douglas's money is lost?"

"Every farthing of it, worse luck!"

"And are they badly off?"

"I'm afraid they are, Ken. I'm very much afraid they are. I'm awfully sorry about it."

There was silence for some minutes, and then the old man said feebly—

"Ken, I've been a good father to you."

"Yes, indeed you have."

"Now, I want you to make me a promise."

"What is it, father?"

"I want you to promise that you'll go and see Mrs. Douglas when I'm dead, and tell her about it."

"Can't I write to her?"

"No; I want you to see her, and break it gentle-like to her, and tell her I was sorry. Be sure and tell her that, Ken."

"I could write all that, father?"

The old man's natural impatience returned. "Can't you do what I tell you?" he said.

"It won't be pleasant to tell her, father—most unpleasant, I should say."

"Never mind, I've done lots of unpleasant things for you, as you'll know some day. Promise, Ken."

"Well, father, if it will be any comfort to you, I'll promise, but I would much rather not go on such an errand."

But old Mr. Fortescue had got the promise that he wanted, and he knew that the Captain was a man whose word could be depended upon.

"Ring for Watson now, Ken."

She came in, and began to bustle about the room, putting things straight for the night.

"Are you going to sit up, Watson?"

"Yes, of course," she said shortly; "the master can't be left."

The Captain noticed that she omitted the usual "sir" in speaking to him; but Watson's bad temper was well-known to him, and he was not surprised.

"Call me, Watson, if I can be of any use."

But Watson pretended not to hear, and began putting coal on the fire, and noisily rattling the fire-irons as she did so. The old man had closed his eyes, and was apparently fast asleep. So the Captain crept out of the room and softly closed the door behind him.

On the landing outside, he found the old butler.

"How is the master, sir?"

"No worse, I think, Elkington; he seems to be sleeping now. My old room, I suppose?"

"Yes, sir; your bag is there."

"Good night, Elkington."

"Good night, sir. I hope you'll find all comfortable."

CHAPTER IV
A TROUBLED NIGHT

IT was not, however, a good night, as far as Kenneth Fortescue was concerned, for he found it utterly impossible to sleep. Was it surprising that this should be the case, after the agitating day that had gone before it? The startling telegram from home, the suspense during the journey, the unexpected meeting with his friends in Birmingham, the sad news on arriving home of his father's illness—the remembrance of all these kept sleep far away from him.

And then there was the cause of that illness—the ruin which had befallen all his hopes and prospects. How could he continue in the army, if his father were correct in saying that all his money was lost? It would be impossible! He was not an extravagant man; but he knew that, with the greatest care and economy, he could not live upon his captain's pay. What, then, could he do? What would become of him? What future could possibly be in front of him?

Then his thoughts travelled to the mysterious envelope which lay in the safe in the next room. What would he find when he opened it? What revelation for him did it contain?

His father had said something about money belonging to himself, which had been lost with the rest; he had never known that he possessed any. Could it be money settled on his mother, which reverted to him at her death? If so, why was he never told of this? Why was it not handed over to him when he came of age? Could there be wrongdoing on his father's part of which he as yet knew nothing?

Then more troubled thoughts still distracted him and kept him long awake. He thought of poor Mrs. Douglas—a widow with a family dependent upon her—and then of the awful news which he had to break to her—news which made him ashamed of his own father. What business had he to put trust money—for surely that insurance money was that in reality—into such a risky concern as a South American gold mine? How could his father have been so foolish—he had almost said so wicked; but, inasmuch as all the old man's own money was invested in the same concern, he gladly altered the adjective to foolish. How should he ever tell her? How could he possibly soften down so hard and terrible a blow? What could he say to let her know how much he felt for her? He would always look upon that four thousand pounds as a debt that he owed to her and to her family. If not legally bound to repay her, he felt that morally he was responsible. Yet how could he possibly do it? He knew not how to provide for his own wants in the future, much less how to be able to save so large a sum.

Then he thought of the poor old man, dying in the next room; that he was dying, he had very little doubt. There was a look in his face which he had never seen there before, and he knew what that look meant—the soul was striving to escape from the poor worn-out body. And where was that soul going? Was his father ready for the great change so close upon him?

It was only lately that Captain Fortescue had felt the all-importance of knowing that the soul is safe for Eternity. But his regiment had been ordered out to the war, and, on the eve of a great battle, he was resting in his tent when three officers rode past it. They pulled up close to where he was, and stood still looking at the sunset, which was a very glorious one that evening. One of them—the eldest of the three—said as he looked across the valley at the long lines of the enemy—

"I wonder where we three will be when the sun sets to-morrow evening?"

The man next him laughed, and said lightly, "Who cares? A short life and a merry one for me!"

"What do you say?" asked the senior officer, turning to the young lieutenant, who was riding on the other side of him.

As Fortescue lay in his tent, with the door open to the west, he could see the young officer, whom he had known at Sandhurst, looking steadfastly at the fast-setting sun; and he could hear him say softly, almost as if he were speaking to himself—

> "Peace, perfect peace; my future all unknown.
> Jesus I know, and He is on the Throne."

The next evening came, and the sunset was as fine as the night before, but the golden rays were streaming down upon a bloody battlefield covered with the dead and dying. The Major who had asked that question of his companions was riding across the valley, but he was riding alone; for his two friends were lying amongst the dead, cold and still. Fortescue saw him, and he knew that he alone of the three was left to see the sun go down. And, as he looked, he envied the young lieutenant who had met death with such calm confidence. Perhaps the next battlefield might be his own last resting-place. Who knew? And as he knelt in his tent that night to say his prayers he had asked that that perfect peace might be his also; and now he, too, could say—

"Jesus I know, and He is on the Throne."

But could his poor old father say that? He was afraid not. He felt that he ought to speak to him, but it would be very difficult.

The Captain was naturally a very reserved man; he would have found it extremely difficult to speak to any one on such a subject, but to say anything of the kind to his old father seemed to him a task which he dared not undertake. Perhaps he could persuade him to see a clergyman to-morrow; he could, at any rate, venture to suggest that he should do so.

And so at last morning dawned, and, thoroughly wearied by the many troubled thoughts of the night, Captain Fortescue got up and dressed. But before he went downstairs, he crept into his father's room and stood by his bed. Watson had gone to the kitchen for something she wanted, and he found no one in the room. The old man's eyes were closed, and he thought he was asleep. But he opened his eyes after a time, and looked at his son.

"Kenneth," he said.

"Yes, father. I came to see how you are."

"Remember your promise."

"I won't forget."

"I'm very ill, Kenneth."

"I'm afraid you are, father. Won't you let me send for the clergyman to come and see you?"

"No, Kenneth—no. I don't know him. He's only just come here. He did call once, but I was out."

There were a few minutes' silence after this, and then he said:

"Couldn't you talk to me a bit, Ken? You know more of these things than I do. I want—I want—"

"You want to know where you are going, father; that's it, isn't it?"

"Yes, that's it, Ken. It's all dark-like, and I've not been what I ought to ha' been."

"We have erred and strayed from Thy ways like lost sheep. We have left undone what we ought to have done, and have done that which we ought not to have done, and there is no health in us."

"That's it, Ken," said the old man; "that's just it!"

"But the Lord Jesus came to save the lost sheep, father. He will save you, if you ask Him. He died for sinners, you know."

"Yes, Kenneth, yes; but I don't know how to ask Him. What shall I say?"

"Say this, father—

> "'Just as I am without one plea,
> But that Thy Blood was shed for me,
> And that Thou bidd'st me come to Thee,
> O Lamb of God, I come.'"

The old man repeated the words after his son, and many and many a time during the day, as Captain Fortescue sat beside him, he heard him saying softly—

"O Lamb of God, I come."

Kenneth Fortescue never went to bed that night, he sat holding his dying father's hand.

Watson did her best to get rid of him, but in vain; he insisted upon remaining where he was. The old butler also crept into the room, and sat watching his master from the foot of the bed.

And, just as the first morning light came streaming through the window, the Captain heard the old man say for the last time—

"O Lamb of God, I come."

And the next minute all was still, and their long watch was ended.

CHAPTER V
THE SAFE OPENED

BEFORE Captain Fortescue left his father's room that morning, he took up the bunch of keys on which the old man's eyes had rested with such anxious care, and which were still lying on a small table near his bed. He slipped them at once into his pocket, for he did not know who might come into that room, and he wished to feel assured that the safe would not be tampered with.

But, eager though he was to discover what secret the letter addressed to him contained, it was not until late in the day that he went into the room of death, that he might open the safe, and find the envelope which his father had described to him. He had been much moved by his father's death; and, in his intense refinement of feeling, he shrank from too quickly bringing to light that which might possibly reveal to him something in his father's past life, which would bring discredit on his memory, and might cause him to think less kindly and tenderly of the dead.

It was the old man's intense anxiety that the paper should not be read in his lifetime, which led Captain Fortescue to surmise that the contents were in some way not creditable to him.

But in the evening, when all arrangements for the funeral were made, and the servants were below at their supper, he crept with a candle in his hand into the room of death. He felt almost as if he were a thief, as he crossed the floor, and passed the silent form on the bed.

His father had never allowed any one to open that safe. In the days of his childhood he had been accustomed to look at it with awe and wonder, as he speculated on the mysteries it might contain. Now—he was going to open it, and the hand that had so carefully guarded its contents was lying cold and lifeless on the bed. He felt almost as if he would hear his father's protesting voice, as he fitted the key in the lock. He even glanced back at the bed, as if to assure himself that there was no movement there.

The lock turned easily, and the massive iron door flew open. As he looked inside, he saw several packets of deeds tied up with red tape, a pile of account books, and countless old chequebooks. But he did not stop to look carefully at what the safe contained, his eyes sought eagerly for the will, for had not his father told him that, underneath that will, he would find the secret information that he wished him to receive?

HE TURNED ROUND AND SAW WATSON STANDING BEHIND HIM.

Yes, the will was there; he saw the large envelope on which was written, in clear legal copper-plate characters, "Last Will and Testament of Joseph Fortescue." But the will had little interest for him now. Of what avail to be told that so many thousands had been bequeathed to him, when he knew that those thousands did not exist, but had been swamped in the ruinous flooding of that distant mine? As his poor old father had said, the will was not worth the paper on which it was written. He took it up with beating heart, and looked underneath it.

Yes, there was the letter; he could see his father's crooked, illiterate writing upon it—he could read the words—

"For my son,
To be opened after my death."

He was just slipping it into his pocket, when he heard a movement in the room. Was the dead man rising, to make a protest against his reading its contents?

He turned round and saw Watson standing behind him; how she had crept into the room without his hearing her he could not imagine.

"What do you want, Watson?"

"I was passing the door, sir, and saw a light, so came in to see that all was right. You've soon found your way to the safe, sir!"

Captain Fortescue took no notice of this insolent remark; he was not going to give vent to his feeling of anger in the chamber of death; he knew that he would have another opportunity of letting Watson know what he thought of her behaviour to him. So, without deigning to reply, he locked the safe, and taking the will and the keys in his hand he went out of the room.

Crossing the landing, he entered his own bedroom, and closed and locked the door. Now he was safe from intrusion and from Watson's prying gaze. He put his candle on the table, drew a chair near it, and sat down to open the letter. He wondered at himself that he could wait even to do this; but he had a nervous dread of the revelation he was about to receive, and, at the last moment, he actually feared to look upon that which before he had been so anxious to see.

He tore open the long envelope, which was securely fastened at one end, and drew out a sheet of foolscap paper.

He opened it and spread it before him; he turned over the page; he looked at the back of it.

Horror of horrors! Had sudden blindness fallen upon him? Was the loss of sight to be added to all his other losses? He could see nothing—not a single word appeared to be written on any one of the four pages. So far as he could see, it was simply a blank sheet, unused, unsoiled, utterly void of any information on any subject whatever. He held it up to the light; he tried to imagine that he saw secret marks in the tracing of the paper; he turned the pages over and over, but he could find nothing but emptiness—a plain, white surface which seemed to mock his scrutiny.

Surely he had brought the wrong envelope! But no, there was the address on the outside in his father's childish handwriting:

"For my son,
To be opened after my death."

Could the old man have made a mistake, and have placed the wrong document in the cover?

He went back to the room of death, carefully locking the door this time, and he made a thorough investigation of the contents of the safe. But he found nothing whatever to repay his search, no other envelope, no other letter—nothing at all but old accounts and a few business papers.

He stood by the bed and looked at his dead father's face, and longed unutterably to ask him what he had done with the information which he had so much wished him to receive. But the lips were closed—the voice was still—and no message came from the other world to guide and direct him in his time of bewilderment and consternation. Fortescue went to his bedroom again, and once more examined the sheet of paper. Then a bright thought seized him. Could it be that his father, fearing lest the document should fall into other hands, had written it in invisible ink? Was it possible that, if he only knew how to deal with it, he might be able to fill those blank pages with words of weight and importance? He remembered, when he was a boy, having a bottle of ink of that kind, which made no mark upon the paper unless heat were brought to bear upon it. Perhaps his father had remembered it also, and, recollecting the fact that he had known the secret as a boy, he had adopted this means of making his letter even more private, and had thus considerably lessened the liability of its being deciphered by any eyes excepting those of his son.

Captain Fortescue therefore went into the library, and carefully held the foolscap sheet to the fire. But, beyond a slight mark of scorching upon one page, it remained unchanged and exactly as he had found it.

Then it crossed his mind that possibly there might be chemicals, which, if applied to paper which had been prepared in a certain way, would bring to light hidden writing and make it legible. He thought he had read of something of the kind being used in time of war, in the place of the ordinary cipher. Possibly this was the explanation which he was seeking. He rang the bell, and Elkington answered it.

"What time do the shops close, Elkington?"

"Eight o'clock, sir."

The captain looked at his watch. "A quarter past nine! Too late, then!"

"What am I thinking of?" said the old butler. "Of course, it's Saturday night. They won't close till ten, or eleven, maybe."

"That's right. Can you send for a cab for me, Elkington?"

"Is it anything I can do, sir?"

"No, Elkington, thank you. I'm afraid not."

"Do you want the cab at once, sir?"

"Yes, at once. The sooner the better."

The old man hurried off to do his young master's bidding, and Kenneth, after placing the precious sheet of paper carefully in the breast pocket of his coat, stood waiting in the hall until the cab arrived. He saw Watson come to the top of the stairs and look down, as if she were watching his movements. Then she came into the hall.

"Are you going out, sir? So late, too?" she added.

The cab drove up at this moment, so that he did not deem it necessary to answer, but he saw her craning her neck forward, that she might catch the direction that he gave to the cabman. Consequently, he altered what he had intended to say, merely naming the part of the town to which he wished to be driven.

The streets of Sheffield were brilliantly lighted as he drove through them; crowds of working people were thronging the main thoroughfares and filling the various shops. But the large chemist's, at which he told the cabman to stop, was practically empty, and the assistants were preparing to close for the night.

"Is Mr. Lofthouse here?" he inquired of one of them.

"He is in his private room, sir. I'll call him. You are only just in time to catch him!"

"Do you think I could speak to him for a few minutes on a private matter?"

"I'll ask him, sir."

In a few moments Kenneth found himself seated beside the old chemist, near the fast-dying embers of the fire in the room behind the shop. He brought the sheet of paper from his pocket and explained his errand. He told Mr. Lofthouse that this paper contained, at least so he believed, information of grave importance to him, and that, whilst it was impossible for him to read it at present, he suspected and hoped that the action of some chemical might be sufficient to bring the writing upon it to light.

The chemist looked carefully at his visitor. Was he a lunatic who was labouring under some strong delusion, or had he good reason for imagining that those blank pages really contained hidden writing? It struck him as a strange time for such a visit, and that made him inclined to be suspicious of the sanity of the man before him. But the Captain's calm, quiet manner impressed him favourably, and when he presently took Mr. Lofthouse into his confidence, by telling him that a relative of his who had lately died had informed him on his death-bed that this paper contained information which it was important for him to receive, he became at once interested and at the same time eager and ready to help.

He inquired whether Captain Fortescue would be willing to entrust the paper to his care, that he might be able to experiment upon it; but when he found that Kenneth did not like the idea of doing so, inasmuch as the information which he supposed the foolscap sheet to contain was of a private nature and intended only for his own perusal, Mr. Lofthouse at once dismissed his assistants, locked the shop door, took his visitor into the laboratory, and proceeded to try the effect of various chemicals upon the paper which he had brought.

For more than an hour the two men worked away on the mysterious pages, but at the end of that time the old chemist declared his firm conviction that the captain was in some way mistaken, for that nothing whatever had been written upon the sheet of foolscap. He could find no evidence of the paper having been chemically treated, and he felt sure that, in some way or other, that paper had been placed in the envelope in the place of the paper which Captain Fortescue had expected to find there.

It was late at night when Kenneth returned home; he was more tired than he realized, until he found himself in his own room, and he slept soundly for the first time since his arrival in Sheffield.

Then followed the long quiet Sunday, during which he sat in the darkened library, and thought of the changes that week had brought into his life, and of the uncertain and difficult future that lay ahead of him.

The funeral was fixed for Tuesday; there were no relations to summon, for he knew of none. He never in his life remembered seeing any one except his father who could claim any relationship to him, however distant. And now that only relation of his was gone, and he was left entirely alone in the world, so far as any natural tie was concerned.

Not only so, but he realized that that week he had lost all his former friends. The schoolfellows at Eton, the men he had known at Sandhurst, the friends he had made since he had entered the army, would now be parted from him by a social gulf which neither he nor they would be able to cross. He would have to sever his connection with them all; leaving the army, he would leave the link which bound him to them. He must begin life anew, and it must be, in future, the life of a man dependent upon his own exertions for his daily bread. How he was to enter upon this life, how that daily bread was to be obtained, he had no idea; what path he could cut out for himself in the hard rock of circumstances which blocked his way, he could not imagine. Nor did he know to whom to apply for advice; his friends were moving in such a totally different sphere that he did not see how they could help him. He felt utterly and entirely alone.

But, at that moment, there suddenly flashed across him four lines which he had learnt to love in brighter and happier days, but which now came back to him with fresh meaning, as they seemed to express the inmost feeling of his heart:

> "I do not ask my cross to understand,
>   My way to see:
> Better in darkness just to feel Thy hand,
>   And follow Thee."

CHAPTER VI
THE TWO ENVELOPES

CAPTAIN FORTESCUE followed his father to the grave, the chief and only mourner. No one else was present, except Mr. Fortescue's doctor and lawyer, who came in their official capacity. The extensive town cemetery looked the very picture of desolation and gloom. It lay in a narrow valley, the rising ground on either side and the stretch of lower ground between being densely covered with the resting-places of the dead.

In the quiet village churchyard, with its green mounds and neat flower-covered graves; its pure white marble crosses and the moss-covered headstones of earlier date; its neat well-kept paths, by the side of which are growing snowdrops and primroses planted by loving hands which are now, it may be, themselves lying in one of those newer mounds; the grave is robbed of some of its outward ghastliness and nakedness, and is clothed tenderly by the loving hand of mother earth.

But in this large town cemetery everything is unsightly and depressing, and the hosts of barren graves, which may be counted by their thousands, are marked only by blackened stones, upon which layer after layer of furnace smoke has settled, and is still settling as the years go by. No flowers will grow there, no trees will thrive; even the scanty grass is more black than green, whilst down in the hollow there lies, at the further end of the valley, a dismal pond, in which the body of a poor suicide was found not so long ago, and the memory of whom leaves an additional shadow upon that melancholy and dismal place.

"Earth to earth; dust to dust; ashes to ashes;" and so the poor earthly remains were left behind, and another leaf was added to the great heap of fallen leaves in the forest of mortal humanity.

When Captain Fortescue arrived home, and walked into the empty house which he would never again call home, he felt as if he were crossing the threshold of the life of hardship which lay in front of him. He determined, however, to face it bravely, and in higher strength than his own, and not to flinch from any duty, however unpleasant, which lay along its course.

In the strength of this resolution, he rang the bell, as soon as his solitary dinner was over, and requested all the servants to assemble in the library, as he had something which he wished to say to them.

He went in, carrying his father's will in his hand, and then he told them that he felt that it was only right they should know that their old master had remembered their faithful service, and had intended rewarding it by a handsome legacy, the amount of which was regulated by the length of time each had lived with him; but that it was his sad and painful duty to inform them that the whole of his father's invested money had been lost, and that therefore, he feared that these legacies existed merely in name.

"Do you mean to tell us, sir, that we shall get nothing?" inquired Watson.

"I fear not, Watson; time alone will show. My father's lawyer, Mr. Northcourt, who was here to-day, is winding up his affairs, of which I know practically nothing, and should there turn out to be money available, of course the legacies will be paid."

"It's very hard, sir, to be turned adrift after all these years!"

"It is hard, Watson; but you must remember I am a sufferer as well as you; it is very hard for me."

Watson gave a sniff of contempt. "You have your commission, sir, and your grand friends."

"Say had, Watson, not have; all that will be a thing of the past. I must leave the army."

"Dear, dear!" said the old butler. "Dear, dear! I do feel for you, sir."

"But surely," said Watson, "there will be something. Look at all this furniture, and the house and park; they haven't gone!"

"Yes, there may be something, Watson. I can't tell yet until I know what my father's obligations were. I fear that he was more than an ordinary shareholder in this mine, and that those who have lost by means of it may come upon his estate for such compensation as it may be able to yield. You may rest assured, however, that your legacies will be paid before I myself touch a single penny of my father's money."

"It's very good of you to say so," said the old butler; "but I'm sure none of us would like to rob you, sir."

"It would be no robbery, Elkington, only justice," said the Captain.

"Well, it's very hard!" said Watson. "Very hard; and what's to become of me, I'm sure I don't know. I can't take another situation at my time of life, and the old gentleman always promised he'd see I was provided for."

"Again I say, Watson, I am very sorry; I can't say more."

"And now there is something else I want to say to you," added the Captain, as he folded up the will; "and I would ask you to give very serious attention to what I am about to tell you. My father informed me, the day before he died, that he had addressed a letter to me, and had put it in the safe in his bedroom with his will. That letter I have never received. The envelope was there, addressed in my father's handwriting, but when I opened it, it contained nothing but a blank sheet of paper. Now I am convinced that that envelope has been tampered with by some one. I am certain that it has been opened, that the paper my father expected me to find there has been removed, and that the blank sheet has been inserted in its place, and I want you to help me to discover how and when this was done, and by whose hands. Elkington, do you know where my father kept the keys of his safe?"

"The old master always had them about him, sir, day and night, as you might say. He carried them in his pocket by day, and at night they were either under his pillow or on the table by his bed. Did you ever know him leave them about, or forget them?"

"Never, sir, never once. He were as careful of these keys, and kept them as well within his reach as a cat does a mouse she has caught; he seemed always to have an eye on them."

"Well, then, we come to the day of his sudden seizure when the telegram was brought in. Where were his keys then?"

"In his pocket, sir. I know he had them, for the post-bag was brought up from the lodge a few minutes before, and I took it to him, and he brought the keys out of his pocket to open it."

"And put them back again?"

"Oh yes, sir, he never forgot to do that."

"Well, then the doctor came, and what happened next?"

"He was carried upstairs, sir. Dr. Cholmondeley helped us, and then we got him into bed."

"Who did?"

"The doctor, and me, and Watson."

"Where were the keys then?"

"Left in the pocket of his coat, sir; but, as soon as ever he came round a bit and opened his eyes, he asked for them; it was almost the first thing he said."

"And where did you put them?"

"On the table where you saw them, sir, close to his bed. They were there, as far as I know, till you took them away."

"Just after the old master breathed his last," ejaculated Watson.

"Now," said Captain Fortescue, "it seems to me we are getting the question into a very small compass. My father was taken ill early in the morning; for a short time those keys were left in his pocket. How long, Elkington?"

"About an hour, sir, I should say."

"Well, either at that time, or some time during the following night, some one must have gone to the safe and taken out my letter."

"How dare you speak like that?" shrieked Watson, "suspecting and accusing your poor father's faithful servants. I suppose you mean I'm the thief, or Elkington?"

"I accuse nobody, Watson. I only ask for an explanation of what is so mysterious to me."

But Watson bounced out of the room, saying she was not going to stay there to be called a common thief; she should pack her box that very night, and get away from a house where she was so insulted.

The servants filed out of the room, but the old butler lingered behind.

"Sir," he said, "do you think that that woman has done it?"

"Elkington, I have no proof, and therefore I do not like to say that any one has done it. It may have been a mistake on my father's part."

"Not likely, sir, not likely; he was so slow and careful-like about things of that sort."

"Well, Elkington, I don't know what to think."

"I do know what to think," said the old butler to himself, as he went out of the room.

But the next day a solution of the mystery came to light. It was late in the evening, and when Elkington was waiting at dinner, that there was a loud ring at the front door. He went to open it, for, now Watson was gone, he was doing most of her work as well as his own. He came back with a card in his hand, which he said had been given to him by a gentleman who had just called, and who was now in the library.

"I told him you were at dinner, sir, but he said he would wait, as he particularly wished to see you to-night."

Captain Fortescue looked at the card. It was not a visiting card, but one evidently used as a tradesman's advertisement. It bore these words, printed in various styles of type—

"JOSIAH MAKEPEACE,
Bookseller and Stationer,
149, York Street,
Sheffield."

"Do you know this man, Elkington?"

"What's his name, sir?"

"Makepeace; he is a bookseller in the town."

"I've heard of him, sir; his shop is in York Street, isn't it?"

"Yes; 149, York Street."

"I believe my master dealt there sometimes. I think I remember seeing his name on parcels that came. Paper and such-like, I think they were."

"He has probably brought his bill, then, and wants to make sure he is paid before others come in for the spoil. Tell him I will see him in a few minutes, Elkington."

When Fortescue entered the library the man was standing with his back to him, gazing at the portrait of Mrs. Fortescue, which hung over the chimney-piece. He was a tall thin man, with black hair, and, as he turned round on his entrance, the Captain could see that his face was sallow, that he had a short beard and small rat-like eyes, and that he was wearing spectacles.

"Good evening, sir. I hope you will excuse my intruding at this hour, but I come on a matter of importance."

Captain Fortescue motioned him to a chair, and said he supposed it was a business matter which had brought him there.

"Not exactly, sir. Your father did do business with me at times, and it is in connection with one of these times that I want to see you. The fact is that a letter, which Mr. Fortescue wrote to you last week, has, by some mistake, come into my hands."

Kenneth looked eagerly at the envelope which Makepeace drew out of the breast pocket of his coat. What revelation did it contain? And how unfortunate that that revelation should have fallen into the hands of a stranger!

The envelope was a foolscap one, he could see that; precisely similar to the one he had found in the safe.

He stretched out his hand for it eagerly.

"Wait a minute, sir," said the man. "Allow me, if you please, to explain to you how this letter came into my possession. Last week—it would be Wednesday, I think—your father came into my shop; it was the last time, I believe, that the old gentleman was out.

"'Makepeace,' he said, 'I want some foolscap paper.'

"My assistant brought some out and showed it to him. We have some blue and some white. He selected the white, sir, but when he looked at it, he declared that it was poorer in quality than what he had bought of me before. I told him that could not be the case, inasmuch as I had bought it all from the same firm and at the same time. Well, he seemed very much put out, and he shouted and stormed at me; it was a way he had, you know, sir, and he wanted to make out I was trying to impose on him by giving him different paper.

"I didn't want to offend the old gentleman, for he was a good customer, so I told him if he would send me a sheet of the foolscap which I had sold him before, I felt sure that I could match it exactly. I meant to give him what I had in stock, for I knew it was exactly the same, but I thought this would satisfy and pacify him. Well, he came round after that, and said he knew I always did the best I could for him, and he told me he would slip it into an envelope as soon as he got home and send it to me by post. On Thursday the letter arrived, but I was from home, and my wife was away too. I've only got a young assistant, and he did not like to open my letters, so there it remained on my desk until I got home to-day."

"And then you opened it?"

"Yes, and found inside, not the sheet of foolscap as I expected, but a letter evidently intended for you, sir. It begins, 'My dear Ken,' and it ends 'Your loving Father.' I haven't read it, sir, I assure you. I wouldn't do such a thing, and I've brought it at once to you. Do you think he can have put it in the wrong envelope? Have you found any other envelope containing a blank sheet of foolscap paper?"

"Yes, I have," said Captain Fortescue, "and have been extremely puzzled by it, for my father expressly told me that he had written a letter which he particularly wished me to receive."

"Then I am only too glad to restore it to you, sir," said Makepeace, as he handed the envelope to him. "And now, sir, I will bid you good evening."

Captain Fortescue thanked him for taking the trouble to come up at once to see him, and assured him that the information which he had given him was an intense relief to his mind.

As soon as he was alone, he unfolded the letter which had at last come into his possession. His hand trembled as he did so, and as he wondered what disclosure it would make to him.

Yes, there was his father's uneven writing. Some of the capitals were printed, others written in the ordinary way. He began at once to read it. It was dated Wednesday, December 18, and ran as follows:

> "MY DEAR KEN,
>
> "I was glad to get your letter, and hope as this will find you well as it leaves me very middling, and Cholmondeley has given me a tonic, so hope soon to be better. There is something as I think you ought to be told, as it will come more easy to you if things goes wrong, as it seems likely they will. I have had a letter from Berkinshaw, a friend of mine in London, and he has found out that a certain concern, what I put my money in, is getting shaky and not likely to pay. So I'm going to sell out to-morrow, unless I hear better news from him by the morning post, and if I do sell out, I shan't be so flush of money by a long chalk, and that will mean I can't send you such a big allowance as you have been having. I thought it was better as I should tell you, in case you might be disappointed when I send your next cheque. Go easy then, and don't outrun the constable till you hear again from—
>
> "Your loving father,
>
> "JOSEPH FORTESCUE."

And that was all! There was not a word more! It all seemed such past history now. And moreover his father had told him a great deal more than this letter contained. Why, then, was he so anxious for him to receive it? What did he mean by saying that he hoped it would put him right, and that he was to follow it up? Could his father simply have meant that this letter would prove that, whatever roguery there might be in connection with the Brazil Mining Company, his son knew nothing at all about the concern, and could not therefore be held in any way responsible? Yet who would ever imagine, for a moment, that he was implicated in his father's business transactions, which were done when he was absent from home, and of which he could easily prove that he was in total ignorance?

Then again, it seemed strange that the letter had never been posted. Why had he not received it on the Thursday morning? He could quite understand that it was possible for his father, having addressed the two envelopes at the same time, to have put the wrong enclosure in each; thus sending the letter to his son to Makepeace, and at the same time forwarding to himself the blank sheet of foolscap intended for the bookseller. But supposing this to have been the case, why, then, were not both letters posted? Why was one sent and the other kept back? And why, being kept back, was the letter placed in the safe?

The Captain meditated for a long time over this difficult question, and then attempted to explain it to himself in this way. He supposed that, after the two letters were closed and ready for the post, they lay together on the library table, that after a time some one, probably his father himself, took up the one addressed to Makepeace and put it into the letter-bag; but that the other letter, addressed to himself, was inadvertently left behind and forgotten, being covered up at the time, perhaps, by something on the table.

That subsequently, late at night and after the post-bag had gone to the lodge, his father discovered that he had omitted to post it; and that then, inasmuch as the letter contained matter of a private nature, he did not care to leave it lying on the table, but had carried it up with him to bed, and in accordance with his usual caution and suspicion had placed it in the safe until the morning. That then, on the Thursday, before he had opportunity to post it, the telegram arrived and his sudden illness occurred; and that consequently the letter written the day before was left in the safe; that then he had appeared on the scene, and of course his father, having no longer any occasion to post the letter, had merely called his attention to it and told him where it had been placed.

The Captain went up to bed that night feeling considerably relieved that the communication in the letter was, after all, of so harmless a nature. He had evidently been making much ado about nothing; the so-called mystery had turned out to be most easy of solution and had nothing very mysterious about it.

But as he lay awake thinking of it all, and only half satisfied with the explanation that he had worked out with so much care, two unanswerable problems suggested themselves to him, and made him feel that, after all, he had by no means got to the bottom of the strange occurrence, and that there still remained much that was mysterious and suspicious.

For, in the first place, was it likely that his father, having written a letter to him on ordinary note-paper, would place it, when written, in a foolscap envelope? The very size of the sheet would prevent his making the mistake which he had thought it possible that he might have made.

And, moreover—and this latter problem he felt was by far the greater one—why was the letter to himself addressed in the way it was? Did it not say on the envelope, "For my son—to be opened after my death?" His father would never have addressed it in that way, had he intended to post it.

What did it all mean? His former theory was entirely upset by the remembrance of this fact. He felt that he had not worked out the solution correctly after all.

Kenneth Fortescue's brain felt in a whirl; the longer he puzzled over it, the more hopelessly bewildered he became. All night long he was struggling to find some possible explanation which might prove satisfactory in all points, but he utterly failed to discover one.

Tired in mind and body, he rose in the morning determined to lay the whole matter before his father's lawyer. He went to Mr. Northcourt's office, and took him entirely into his confidence; but neither he nor the lawyer were able to come to any conclusion as to what had happened with regard to the two letters.

The Captain suggested calling in a detective, but Mr. Northcourt dissuaded him from pursuing this course of action, at any rate, for the present, inasmuch as he failed to see proof that there had been foul play in the matter. For, if Makepeace had had any hand, directly or indirectly, in removing the letter from the safe, why was he so anxious and ready to restore it to its rightful owner? However, he promised the Captain that he would lose no opportunity of trying to discover a clue to the mystery, and told him that, if anything came to his knowledge at all bearing upon what had happened, he would not fail to communicate with him immediately.

CHAPTER VII
A WALK THROUGH BORROWDALE

A FEW days later, and during the first week of the new year, Captain Fortescue was once more to be seen at the large railway station in Sheffield. He was doing what he had never done in the whole course of his life before; he was taking a third-class ticket. He was a poor man now, and he felt that he must act as one.

It was a new experience for him to be obliged to pull himself up at every turn when he was on the point of spending little sums of money. Instead of buying, as before, several books and papers at the stall, he contented himself with a copy of one paper only; instead of ordering a luncheon basket, he was carrying in his pocket a small packet of sandwiches which old Elkington had carefully wrapped up for him that morning; instead of coming to the station in a cab, he had made use of a public conveyance.

All this was new and strange to him, and yet he did not mind it in the least; he had endured the hard life in the war without a murmur, and the cessation of these little luxuries was to him a very trivial matter; but he did feel a pang of regret when he had to give the porter a small coin instead of his former generous tip, and when he slipped a penny into the box of the blind man at the station gate, instead of the shilling which he had usually given him when he passed by. He must be just before he was generous, he said to himself.

When the train started, Kenneth Fortescue was soon engrossed in his newspaper; he was glad of anything to turn his thoughts from the errand upon which he was going. For he was on his way into Cumberland to fulfil his promise to his father, and to break the intelligence of her heavy loss to poor Mrs. Douglas. He had had some difficulty in finding her address; he remembered that he had been so filled with horror at his father's disclosure that he had never asked him where she was now living. He had hunted through the old man's papers in vain; he had discovered her address in York, but his father had intimated that she was not there at the present time, and he failed to find any recent address.

However, the old butler, on being questioned, told him that he had several times addressed letters for his master to Mrs. Douglas, and that he could therefore quite distinctly remember her address. He wrote it carefully on a piece of paper, and Captain Fortescue took it from his waistcoat pocket and looked at it more than once during the journey. In the old man's trembling handwriting, he read these words—

"Mrs. Douglas, Fernbank, Rosthwaite,
"nr. Keswick."

Kenneth, much as he wished to get this dreaded visit over, had postponed it until after the new year. He knew that he was the bearer of bad tidings, and, with his usual thoughtfulness for others, he was unwilling that the evil news should come as a cloud across their happiness at Christmas and the New Year.

He had thought once of writing to say that he was coming, but upon second thoughts, he decided not to do so. He would keep his promise to his father to the very letter; he had implored him not to write, and he would therefore refrain from doing so, and would not even prepare them in this way for the sad news which he was bringing to them. He could easily find some place in which to stay the night, and would return to Sheffield early the following morning.

The Captain was alone the first part of the way, but at Penrith a young man jumped into the carriage and took the seat opposite to him. He was short and rather thin, with dark hair, brown eyes, and a weak mouth. There was nothing specially taking in his appearance, and yet he had an extremely good-natured face, which made the Captain imagine that, though his companion might not have a superabundance of brain power, yet at the same time he was well stored with easy good-humour.

The newcomer put his bag on the rack, lighted a cigar, and turned over the leaves of a magazine. But he did not seem much inclined for reading, and soon closed his book and began to talk, opening the conversation, as Englishmen always do, with a remark on the weather.

"Horrid cold day," he said, with a slight drawl, which, however, the Captain soon discovered was a sign of company manners on his part, and which he dropped entirely when they became better acquainted.

"Yes, I think it's the coldest day this winter," he answered; "it feels to me like snow."

"Have some of my rug," said the newcomer. "It's only lying on the ground."

"Thank you, I shall only be too glad; I forgot to bring mine, and the foot-warmer is quite cold now."

"Have you come far?"

"Well, a good way—from Sheffield. I'm going to a little place somewhere near Keswick. Do you know Keswick?"

"Of course I do; I'm going there myself."

"Oh! Then you're the very man I want. I have to get to a village called Rosthwaite; do you know it?"

"Rather! Why, we live only about two miles from Rosthwaite—at Grange, at the lake head."

"Derwentwater is that?"

"Yes, we're at the other end of it from Keswick; it's a pretty long way from the station. Do you know Cumberland?"

"I never was there in my life. Shall I find an inn at Rosthwaite?"

"Oh yes, two of them; they are very comfortable, I believe. Are you thinking of staying at Rosthwaite long?"

"No; I'm only going there on business. I want to find some people who live there. I wonder if you have ever heard of them and can tell me where they live."

"What's the name?"

"Douglas."

"Of course I know the Douglases! I've known them nearly all my life. I spend most of my time there when I'm down—too much, my father says. You see, he wants me to work; but it's an awful grind out of term time. I do a little, of course, but not enough to please him, I'm afraid."

"Are you at Cambridge?"

"No, at Oxford—Magdalen."

"And what are you going to be?"

"Oh! I don't know; anything that's not too hard work. My father says I ought to settle, but it's very hard. Every time I come down, he wants to know if I've made up my mind. But there's time enough yet."

"Don't you think it's better to have an aim in view?"

"Yes, I suppose it is. Oh I shall think of something one of these days. You were asking about the Douglases?"

"Yes; do you mind telling me what you know about them?"

"Not at all. They're jolly, all of them; you're sure to like them!"

"What does the family consist of?"

"Well, there's Mrs. Douglas; he's dead—was a parson, I believe, and had a church in Sheffield—he's been dead years now; we never knew him."

"Is Mrs. Douglas an elderly lady?"

"Oh dear no! She isn't young, but she isn't what you would call elderly; her hair isn't white. Have a cigar?"

"Thank you. And what family has she?"

"Three girls, awfully jolly girls, too; and then there's little Carl."

"I did not think she had any young child."

"No, she hasn't; Carl is Mrs. Douglas's grandchild. Leila is his mother. You see she was only married a few months when she lost her husband, and this little chap was born after his father died, and Leila had to come back home because she was left so badly off."

"Then the girls will be quite grown-up, I suppose?"

"Yes; Phyllis is the youngest, and she's nineteen. Marjorie is my age, our birthdays are on the same day; we shall come of age next month. They're really awfully nice girls! I don't know which I like best, Marjorie or Phyllis; sometimes I think I like one, sometimes the other."

"It's a case of 'How happy could I be with either,'" said Captain Fortescue, laughing. "Fernbank, I think, they live?"

"Yes, it's up on the hill close to the bridge. They have a nice little garden. Leila lies out on her couch in it in summer. She's an invalid now, and has been for months, and they're afraid she'll never be very strong."

"What's the matter with her?"

"Something wrong with her spine, I believe; she looks very ill sometimes. We shall soon be at Keswick now. What do you think of our Cumberland hills?"

"Beautiful!" said the Captain, as he looked out of the window. "Have you had much snow this winter?"

"Yes, a good deal. It's done nothing but rain or snow ever since I came down. Horrid nuisance, too!"

"I'm glad it's fine to-day," said the Captain.

"Yes, if it will only keep so. How are you going to get to Rosthwaite?"

"Are there coaches running there from Keswick?"

"Not in winter; there are plenty in summer."

"Then I must take a cab. How much do they charge?"

It was a new question for Captain Fortescue to have to ask.

"A good bit, I believe; it's a long way, you see. I can give you a lift as far as Grange if you like; the pony trap will be there to meet me."

"It's very kind of you; I shall be most grateful. How far is Grange from Rosthwaite?"

"Oh, a very little way, a short two miles, right through Borrowdale, you know."

When they arrived at Keswick station, the Captain's new friend led the way to the road outside, where they found a pony carriage and a smart-looking groom waiting, and they were soon driving quickly through the streets of the pretty little town.

Then the lake came in sight, beautiful even on that wintry afternoon. A fringe of snow covered the top of Cat Bells and the higher hills on the opposite side of the water, and Derwentwater was lighted up by the rays of the red sun, which had not yet dipped behind their white summits.

Captain Fortescue thought he had never beheld a lovelier scene. The wooded islands with which the lake is studded, the dark fir trees on Friar's Crag, the rocks and trees on the margin of the lake reflected in the still water, the high mountains of Borrowdale shutting out the view before him, and Skiddaw standing in solitary grandeur behind him; all these combined to form a glorious panorama of beauty, on which he gazed with great admiration as he drove along.

His companion talked the whole way, pointing out the different mountain peaks; stopping the carriage that he might hear the roar of Lodore, as its waters, swollen by winter snows, dashed a hundred feet over the precipice; and then, when the lake was left behind, showing him in the distance the beautiful double bridge which crosses the rushing river as it runs towards the lake.

"Do you see those houses," he said, "just in front of us? We are coming to Grange now."

"That is where you live?"

"Yes; in that house on the other side of the river. You can just see the chimneys amongst the trees."

"Then Rosthwaite is two miles further?"

"Not quite two miles; it's a glorious walk!"

"Is there any fear of my losing my way?"

"No; it's quite impossible. Keep straight along the road, and it will take you there."

"Thank you very much. I am most grateful to you for the help you have given me," said the Captain. "May I ask the name of my kind friend?"

"Verner—Louis Verner. My father, Colonel Verner, came to live here ten years ago. And now perhaps you will tell me your name."

"Fortescue. I'm very glad we have met; it has made the last part of my journey very pleasant. Do I get out here?"

"No; wait till we get to the bridge. Why, I do believe that's Marjorie coming across now! Lucky for you if it is; she'll show you the way. Hurry up, Stephens, and we'll catch her before she turns the corner!"

They drove quickly on, and Louis Verner called out to the girl who was nearing the end of the long bridge—

"Marjorie! I say, Marjorie!"

She saw them coming, and waited at the corner, and Louis jumped out of the carriage, followed by the Captain, and went to meet her.

She was wearing a navy blue motor-cap, a coat and skirt of the same colour, and sable furs. She had the brightest, sunniest face, Kenneth thought, that he had ever seen. Her hair was a lovely shade of brown, her eyes were grey; she had a clear complexion, rosy cheeks, and a somewhat Roman nose. All this he remarked afterwards; but at the first glance, he noticed only this—that hers was a face which it did one good to see; one of those thoroughly happy, contented faces which are unfortunately so rare in this world of dissatisfaction and discontent. It was a face which some would not have allowed to be even pretty, and yet, although he could remember having seen faces far more beautiful in feature—Lady Violet's, for instance—he could not recollect having in his whole life seen a single face so lovely in its expression, so vivacious, and so full of intelligence.

"Marjorie, look here! I want to introduce this gentleman to you. Mr. Fortescue—Miss Douglas. He is going to Rosthwaite, and I think he wants to call on Mrs. Douglas."

"Mr. Fortescue!" said Marjorie, in a surprised voice. "Why, I thought—"

"You thought Mr. Fortescue was not quite so young, Miss Douglas; was that it?"

"Yes," she said, laughing. "Mother gets letters sometimes from Mr. Fortescue, and I pictured him a very old man with white hair and spectacles. Why, I don't know; but I always picture people to myself, and often make mistakes."

"That was my father, Miss Douglas; he is dead now."

"Dead! Oh, I'm so sorry," she said. "I should not have said that if I had known."

"Well, Marjorie, will you guide Mr. Fortescue?" said Louis Verner.

"Yes, Louis; I'm going home now, so we can walk together."

When the carriage had driven on, and the Captain found himself alone with Miss Douglas, all the weight of the errand upon which he had come returned upon him. He had tried to forget it for a time; he could not forget it now. She was so bright and cheerful, so anxious to point out to him all the beauties of the scenery through which they were passing, and to make the walk as pleasant to him as she possibly could, that he felt sick at heart when he remembered that his visit would bring a heavy cloud over her life, and drive the sunshine from her face. Why had his father asked him to do this thing?

They were passing through the narrowest part of Borrowdale, where the steep hills confront each other closely in all their rugged beauty. At the bottom of the gorge the river was rushing madly over its rocky bed; overhead towered the mighty Castle Crag, guarding the narrow pass. Every kind of beauty of rock and wood and river, of mossy bank and fern-covered glade, seemed crowded together in that lovely spot.

"What do you think of it, Mr. Fortescue?"

"Glorious!" he said. "How delightful to live amongst it all!"

"Isn't it?" she said. "I don't think I could bear to live in a dirty, smoky town after this. Do you see that great stone above us on the hill—the Bowder Stone it is called. People always go and look at it; but I don't know that there's much to see."

Kenneth did not answer her; the burden of his message was becoming more than he could bear. A sudden thought crossed his mind. Should he tell her why he had come? Perhaps, if he did so, she would help him to think of the best way to tell her mother.

"Miss Douglas," he said, "I suppose you have been wondering why I am going to see your mother?"

"Woman's curiosity, I expect you think! Well, you men are just as curious sometimes. Yes, I did wonder rather what it was about," she said, laughing.

"May I tell you," he answered, so gravely and seriously that her laugh died away, and a look of anxiety came into her face.

"Yes, tell me," she said quietly. "Not bad news, I hope?"

"I'm afraid it is. I'm very much afraid you will think it very bad news."

She waited for him to go on, which he did, speaking with difficulty, for he was touched to see that her colour had faded in a moment. It was a very white face which was turned to him now.

"My father managed a business matter for Mrs. Douglas," he went on. "Your father, when he was dying, asked him to invest some money for her."

"Yes, I know. Mother has often told me how kind he was in doing it for her, and in seeing after it all these years."

"He put the money—your father's insurance money, I believe it was—in India three and a half per cents."

"Yes; mother said it was there."

"It was there."

"Is it not there now?"

"No, not now. My father found what he thought was an exceedingly good investment. He put all his own money into it. Miss Douglas, please remember that—all his own money. And he wanted Mrs. Douglas to share in the good interest that he was receiving, and so he took her money out of the three and a half per cents. and put it in with his own."

"And you have come to tell us it is all lost," she said. She did not say it angrily or bitterly, only very sorrowfully.

"All lost," he repeated. "It was in a mine; the mine is flooded, and has been an utter failure; the shares are not worth a single halfpenny."

"Poor mother! Poor, poor mother!"

"Has she much besides?"

"Not much; there is a little, a very little; but, you see, there's Leila now, and little Carl."

"They live with you?"

"Yes; and little Carl will have to be educated; there is nothing for him whatever, only what mother can do. But how selfish I am!" she went on. "I have been thinking of ourselves, and never thought of you. Won't it make a great difference to you?"

"Yes; of course I shall have to leave the army."

"I didn't know you were a soldier."

"I have just got my captaincy."

"What will you do?"

"I have no idea yet. Go into business, I suppose; but it does not matter about me, if only I could have spared you this awful shock."

"Oh! Please don't think of me," she said, smiling again, though there were tears in her eyes. "I am young and strong and can easily find something to do. Oh! Something is sure to turn up. It is only mother I was thinking of; but I know she will be helped. Please don't trouble about us; it is quite hard enough for you."

"Now, how shall I tell your mother, Miss Douglas?"

"Would it help you if I told her?"

"It would help me very much, but I'm afraid I can't let you do that; you see, I promised my father on his death-bed that I would tell Mrs. Douglas myself."

"Did you? Oh, then you ought to do it, of course."

"When do you think I had better come?"

"Do you mind coming after tea? Leila will have gone to bed then, and I think it would be better for her not to be there. You see, she's a great invalid; but she always goes to bed when little Carl does."

"Shall we say half-past seven, then?"

"Yes, that will do very well. No one will be there but ourselves. Louis comes in most evenings, but he won't come to-night, as he is only just home from Penrith. But won't you come to tea? I'm so sorry, I ought to have asked you before."

"No, thank you. I would rather go straight to the hotel. There are two, I believe; which do you recommend?"

She told him their respective merits, and they settled together to which he should go. And then she talked of the village, and the church, and pointed out the different mountains, and did all she could to put him at his ease again; for she saw how deeply he had felt having to tell her of the heavy loss of which his father had been the cause.

Then they came to a stone bridge which crossed the stream just at the entrance of Rosthwaite. It was almost dark when they got there, but she pointed out the chimneys of her home, standing amongst the trees on the hillside, and then she said good-bye to him in a cheerful voice and went over the bridge, whilst he walked on a few yards further, and found the clean country inn at which he was to spend the night.

CHAPTER VIII
HONISTER CRAG

WHEN Captain Fortescue set out at half-past seven for Fernbank a fearful gale was blowing. The trees rocked and strained overhead, and so violent was the wind, as it came sweeping through the narrow gorge down which he had come that afternoon, that he could hardly fight his way against it, as he attempted to retrace his steps as far as the bridge.

It was a terribly cold night, the ground was as hard as iron, and the bridge was so slippery that he stumbled as he crossed it.

He followed the path beyond, which wound steeply up the hillside, and climbed towards the house, guided as he did so by the lights in the windows. He wondered whether she had told them that he was coming. Perhaps she had, and they were expecting him fearfully, trying to conjecture what news he had come to bring them. But no; on second thoughts, he felt sure that she would not tell them, lest they should ask her whether she knew what his errand was.

He found the garden gate with difficulty, for it was a very dark night, and began to ascend the steep path leading towards the front of the house. This path took him past a bow window, the blind of which was only partly drawn down.

He only glanced at this window for a single moment, turning his eyes away immediately, but in that one glance he had taken in the whole scene, and it remained imprinted on his memory.

A lady with a sweet, gentle face was sitting at the table, darning stockings by the light of the lamp. On the opposite side of the table, with her back to the window and busily engaged in the same occupation, was his companion of the afternoon, Marjorie Douglas; whilst leaning back in an armchair by the fire, with her feet on the fender and a book in her hand, was a pretty fair-haired girl whom he concluded was the younger sister.

Only one glance—and yet the picture of cosy home comfort impressed itself upon him. He even noticed the bricks and tin soldiers on the floor, left behind by the child who had gone to bed.

And now he had come to bring a blight upon their quiet happiness! Had it been possible, even at the last moment, he would have turned back. But it was not possible, for a promise made to the dead was surely too sacred to be disregarded. Whatever it cost him, that promise must be fulfilled.

He rang the bell, and the door was opened by an elderly servant to whom he handed his card, which she at once carried to her mistress.

"Come in, please, sir," she said, as she opened the door of the room into which he had looked.

All three ladies rose as he entered, and Mrs. Douglas said—

"Are you the son of my husband's old friend in Sheffield?"

He told her that he was, and then informed her of his father's death. When she had expressed her regret for this, he told her, as gently as he could, the sad news that he had to bring her, and gave her the message from the dying bed, telling her at the same time that all his poor father's money had been embarked in the same concern, and assuring her of the old man's deep sorrow at what had occurred. He also told her how he had made him promise to acquaint her of the loss by word of mouth, instead of sending the bad news in a letter.

She listened very quietly, and almost as if she were mentally stunned by the blow that had fallen upon her. For some minutes she did not speak, and then she asked—

"Are you sure there is no hope of recovering anything?"

"None, I'm afraid," said Captain Fortescue. "I wish I could give you any hope, but I fear I cannot. It is hard for you to hear, very, very hard, and oh! How hard for me to tell!"

"I'm sure it is," said Marjorie. "I think it is worse for you than for us."

"Mrs. Douglas, I am a poor man now. I cannot continue in my regiment, and so far no path in life has been opened to me; but I assure you of this— that I shall look upon the four thousand pounds you have lost as a debt binding upon me as long as I live, and that, if God prospers me in the future, every single penny of it shall be repaid. I will not wait, however, until I am able to restore the whole capital, for that I fear will be the work of a lifetime; but I will send you from time to time such money as I am able to save, and I will not allow myself in a single indulgence of any kind whatever until the full amount is in your hands."

"It is very good of you—very noble," she said; "but you must not make such a resolve. You are not to blame for our loss; you yourself have lost still more heavily. I cannot let you sacrifice yourself in that way."

"God helping me, Mrs. Douglas," he answered, as he rose to take leave, "my promise will be kept."

Mrs. Douglas pressed him to stay for supper, but he did not accept her invitation; he felt that they would want to be alone, that they might talk over what had happened. So he said good-bye, and Marjorie went to open the door for him. The wind rushed in with hurricane force as soon as it was opened.

"What an awful night, and how dark!" she said, closing the door again. "I will light the lantern, and go with you to the gate, or you will never find it in this darkness."

He begged her not to come, but she would not listen, and, catching up a shawl from the hall table, wrapped it round her, and went in front of him down the garden path with the lantern in her hand. At the gate she stopped.

"How can I thank you, Miss Douglas?"

"Don't try!" she said, laughing. "Can you find your way now, do you think?"

"Oh yes, quite well. Good-bye. I am off early to-morrow morning."

"Then we shall not see you again?"

"No," he said sadly, "perhaps never again. Birds of ill omen are never welcome—are they?"

"Oh! Don't call yourself that," she said. "Good-bye, Captain Fortescue."

He had left her, and was going towards the bridge, when he thought he heard her calling. He looked back, and saw that she was still standing at the gate with the lantern in her hand.

"Did you call, Miss Douglas?" he asked.

"Yes; I ought not to have brought you back, but I did want to thank you."

"I don't know why you should thank me."

"For being so good to mother," she said; and then she turned round and went up the hill, and he watched the light of her lantern until he saw it pass inside the door of the house.

What a wild night that was! Kenneth Fortescue slept very little, for the wind was howling in the chimneys of the old inn, rattling the badly fitting windows, sweeping down the narrow valley, and tearing with terrific force across the open country beyond. He lay listening to the wind, and thinking many troubled thoughts during the long hours of that wakeful night.

He had ordered a carriage to take him to Keswick in time for the early train, so he jumped out of bed as soon as he was called, and went to the window of his room to look out at the weather. The whole country was covered with deep snow. Mountains, rocks, woods, houses, fields, gardens, were alike arrayed in white robes, pure and spotless, and sparkling in the morning sunshine as if covered with countless diamonds.

When, a little later, he went down to the coffee-room, the landlord came to speak to him.

"I'm afraid, sir, you won't be able to go to-day. There's been a terrible snowstorm, and Borrowdale is blocked. It will be impossible to drive through it."

"Surely it is not so deep as that!"

"Not here, sir, nor for about a mile down the valley; but when you come to the turning in the road at the narrowest part of the valley the snow has drifted there to a fearful depth, and for about half a mile the snow is so deep it would be impossible to get through it. We are shut off from Keswick entirely."

"Won't they clear the road?"

"Well, sir, they'll try to make a way through, but it will be a long job. I'm afraid we shan't get through to-day."

"Then there is no help for it," said the Captain. "I must stay."

"Yes, sir; I'm very sorry you should be so inconvenienced, but I'll do my best to make you comfortable; and it's a beautiful country. If you haven't been here before, you might like to see a little of it, and it's good walking round here and on towards Honister, if you care to take a look round."

Yet Kenneth Fortescue was in no hurry to go out, or to leave the great fire in the large grate. He sat beside it with a paper in his hand, reading at times, and at other times gazing at the blue smoke curling up the chimney. And then, after a while, he stood at the window, gazing absently out into the village street. He had much on his mind that morning, and he felt that even the loveliest scenery failed to beguile him from pursuing the troubled train of thought which he felt impelled to follow. But presently he was recalled from the future to the present by seeing Marjorie Douglas pass the window with a covered basket in her hand. Her face looked to him as bright and cheerful as it had done before he had told her the sad news he had come to disclose; the clouds seemed to have dispersed, and the sunshine to have come back to it.

Kenneth wondered where she was going. He caught up his cap and ran after her, to ask how her mother was, and how she had borne the sad tidings he had brought her.

Marjorie heard him coming behind her, and turned round in the greatest surprise.

"Captain Fortescue, I thought you had gone!"

"No, Miss Douglas; I'm the bad penny, as well as the bird of ill omen," he said. "The fact is, there is a snowdrift in the valley, so I have to stay here till to-morrow."

"How tiresome for you!"

"Yes, it is rather; but I shall see a little more of the country—it looks beautiful this morning. Where are you going, Miss Douglas? Let me carry your basket for you."

"Not until you get your coat," she said. "It's far too cold to stand talking without it."

He ran back for it, and soon rejoined her.

"I am going to Seatoller," she said.

"Who is Toller?"

She laughed very much at this question, and told him that Seatoller was the name of the little hamlet where old Mary lived.

"Do you mind my coming with you, Miss Douglas? It's awfully slow going for a walk alone."

"Not at all. Only take care how you carry that basket, because old Mary's pudding and beef-tea are in it."

"Who is old Mary?"

"She's a dear old woman who lives in one of the cottages at Seatoller. Look across the valley, you can see the white houses of the little place. There are only about six, I think. They are just at the bottom of Honister Pass."

"Do you often go to see her?"

"Whenever I can. We have quite a number of old women here. I think it must be because it is so healthy. They all live to be very old, and they are all friends of mine, so they have to take their turn; but this is old Mary's day."

"How they must look forward to their turn!" he said.

"Yes, I think they do; but I'm afraid none of them will get a turn soon. I'm going away, Captain Fortescue."

"Going away?"

"Yes, from home. We settled that last night. You see, we had a little family council after you had gone, to talk things over. Mother wanted to send Dorcas away—that's our old servant—but I don't think that would do. She is very faithful to mother, and though I think I could do most of her work, still on the whole I think it would make more for mother to do. Dorcas does the washing so well, and she's so useful in every way, and we don't like to send her away, if we can possibly help it, poor old soul!"

"Then what do you mean to do?"

"Well, I don't quite know yet. Go as companion or mother's help, I suppose. I don't think I could get any teaching, because I've never passed any exams. Every one seems to require that now. Louis always brings us the 'Standard' when his father has read it, and we shall look in the advertisements."

"It will be awfully hard for you to go away."

"Oh, I don't know! Yes, I suppose it will rather. But I don't mind, if only they get on all right at home; but I think they ought to, if only Phyllis will take care of mother. I think she will. I believe she will; only, you see, she is the youngest, and I'm afraid we've spoilt her a little. But she's such a dear old girl, and I do think she will try."

"I'm terribly sorry that you should have to go."

"Oh, you mustn't be sorry for me," she said, laughing. "I'm not going to be sorry for myself. I dare say I shall be very happy soon, and if not—well, it really does not matter. It will be all the nicer when I get home for the holidays. Now here we are at old Mary's cottage. I must just run in with her things."

Marjorie took the basket from him and went into the house, and as Captain Fortescue watched her, he wondered what the old woman would do when she missed the bright face and cheerful voice of her friend.

When she came out, she took him up the steep pass, that he might see Honister Crag in the distance, standing out in all its majestic grandeur at the head of the pass. On their left-hand side was the mountain torrent, dashing madly over the rocks, coming down so fast that no frost could stay its course; on their right was moorland, the dead heather thickly covered with snow.

About a mile up the pass the snow became deeper, and they had to turn back, and, passing Seatoller again, they retraced their steps to Rosthwaite. Marjorie never alluded again to her going away, or to the loss of the money;

she seemed anxious that he should forget everything painful, that he might be able to carry back with him a happy memory of her beautiful home.

When Kenneth left her at the garden gate, he went back to the inn feeling more hopeful about the future. If she was determined to face it so bravely and happily, surely he could do the same. Perhaps, after all, there were brighter days in store in that future which he had so much dreaded, and which had seemed such a long vista of darkness opening out before him.

After luncheon, he was sitting over the fire in the coffee-room, looking at a paper two days old, and wondering how he should get through the long solitary evening, when the waiter came in and handed him a letter. It was from Mrs. Douglas, inviting him to spend the evening at Fernbank, and assuring him that he would be conferring a favour upon them by doing so, as in winter they were so shut out front the world beyond the valley that they seldom had the pleasure of meeting any one outside their own little circle of friends in Borrowdale. The invitation was so gracefully worded, as if the obligation were entirely on his side, that the Captain felt he could only send an affirmative answer, nor, if the truth were told, did he desire to send any other.

So at five o'clock, he once more crossed the bridge and climbed the hill to Fernbank.

He was shown into a small drawing-room, plainly furnished, but bearing unmistakable marks of taste and care. A china bowl of fern-like moss stood on the table, in which were snowdrops arranged singly, as if they were growing in it. A flower-stand filled with hyacinths of various colours stood in the window; in one corner of the room ivy was growing in a large flower-pot, and was climbing over the chimney-piece, and hanging in graceful festoons from the over-mantle; whilst a vase filled with Pyrus japonica and yellow jessamine stood on the shelf below, and was reflected in the glass.

They all gave him a welcome, and made him feel that they were glad to see him. There was no allusion made during the evening to what he had told them the day before. The bird of ill omen was treated as if he had been the harbinger of good news. Kenneth had been to many costly entertainments of various kinds, but he thought that the cosiness of that Cumberland tea eclipsed them all. The snow-white cloth, the bright, well-trimmed lamp, the early violets and snowdrops tastefully arranged on a pretty table-centre, the freshly baked scones, the girdle-cakes—a speciality of the Lake district—the crisp oat cake, the honey from the hive in the garden, the new-laid eggs from their own poultry yard—all these combined to make the meal an inviting one, and long afterwards, and when in far different surroundings, Kenneth

Fortescue was wont to recall it with pleasure, and to wonder if he would ever again see a like picture of home comfort.

"You look sleepy, Phyllis," said Marjorie, as they sat down to tea. "You ought to have come with me to Seatoller; it was lovely out to-day."

"What's the good of going out when there's nowhere to go? Besides, I was reading. I wanted to finish that book Louis brought. I never can stop when I'm in the middle of a story."

Mrs. Douglas laughed. "Phyllis is afflicted with deafness at times, Captain Fortescue," she said; "if she is reading, she is stone-deaf the whole time."

Leila had joined them at the table, and little Carl, a pretty boy of three, with fair hair and blue eyes, was seated on a high chair by her side. She looked ill and depressed and spoke very little, but the child was full of life, and amused them all with his baby talk.

After tea they had games and music. Phyllis was very clever at the latter and sang well. She was not at all like her sister, very much prettier most people said, but it was beauty of feature rather than of expression. Kenneth thought she had rather a discontented face, and she moved wearily, when she was asked to do anything by her mother, as though every exertion, however small, cost her an effort.

It was Marjorie who was the life of the party, who saw at a glance what every one wanted, who was ready to run here and there for them all; it was Marjorie who carried Carl up to bed; who picked up her mother's ball of wool when it fell, and who kept her eyes open all the time to see what she could do for others, and how she could help them all. How they would miss her! What a blank there would be, if she left them! What a sad change would come over that bright little home when its chief sunbeam was removed from it!

The pleasant evening came to an end at last, and Kenneth rose to take leave. Then, for the first time, he mentioned the object of his visit to Rosthwaite. As he shook hands with Mrs. Douglas, and thanked her for her great kindness to him, he said in a low voice—

"I shall not forget my promise."

She pressed his hand affectionately as she whispered—

"God bless you!" And he knew the words came from her heart.

Then Marjorie ran for the lantern, for there was not a star in the sky, and she insisted on lighting him to the gate.

"Now it really is good-bye," he said; "the road has been cleared, and I am off early to-morrow—Miss Douglas—"

"Yes, Captain Fortescue."

"I have kept my promise to my poor old father as well as I could."

"You have indeed," she said.

"Now I want you to make me a promise."

"What is it?" she asked.

"I want you to let me know as soon as your plans are settled where you are going and what you are going to do. Will you?"

"Yes; I will."

"You won't forget your promise, I know. Good-bye."

History seemed to repeat itself, for, as on the night before, he heard her calling him when he had gone a few steps along the road.

"How can I let you know, when I don't know your address?" she said.

"Of course, I quite forgot I was leaving Sheffield."

He took out a card, and by the light of her lantern, he wrote on it the name and address of his father's lawyer.

"That will always find me," he said. "Once more good-bye."

Again he stood at the gate as she climbed the hill, and when once more, he watched her go into the lighted hall and close the door behind her, he thought that the night looked darker and more dreary than before.

CHAPTER IX
A FINISHED CHAPTER

CAPTAIN FORTESCUE was up early the following morning, and set off in good time for the morning train.

On his way to Keswick, he passed Louis Verner in Borrowdale, and stopped the carriage to speak to him. Louis told him that he had tried to get through the valley the day before, but had found the road quite impassable. He said he was on his way to Fernbank to take Mrs. Douglas the "Standard."

The journey was a cold one, and the Captain was not sorry to reach Sheffield. He had wired the time of his arrival to Elkington, and he found a bright fire in the library, and drawing his chair near it, he opened the pile of letters which had arrived during his absence from home.

Most of these were bills of his father's, but he came to one in a lady's handwriting and with a coronet on the envelope. He opened it, and found that it was a very kind note from Lady Earlswood, telling him that she had seen in the "Times" the notice of his father's death, and that she wished to express her deep sympathy with him in his bereavement. She also wished to invite him to come to Grantley Castle on his way back to Aldershot. The house-party had broken up, but Evelyn was still at home, and they would all be delighted to see him for as long as it was possible for him to stay.

He sat down after dinner to write an answer to this letter, in which he thanked Lady Earlswood for her kindness, but at the same time politely declined her invitation.

He had finished this letter, and was putting it in the envelope which he had addressed, when he suddenly changed his mind, tore up what he had written, and wrote another letter. He would go to see them, and would explain his altered position; it would be better so, and if they chose to drop his acquaintance after they knew all, they could do so. Berington, he thought, would always remain his friend, at least he hoped so; but he was not so sure what Lady Earlswood's view of the subject might be. She was a thorough woman of the world, and might not care to have him at her house when she knew how greatly his prospects had altered.

In a week's time, Kenneth had wound up his father's affairs, as far as it was possible for him to do so, had dismissed the servants and taken an affectionate farewell of the old butler, and had started on his journey to Grantley Castle. As he stepped that afternoon into the brougham waiting for him at the station, he felt as if he were beginning to read the very last page of the first volume of his life.

A five miles' drive took him to the entrance to the Castle, which stood on the side of a hill several hundred feet above sea-level. He drove in at the great gates, which were opened by the lodge-keeper as the carriage was heard approaching. The drive was made through a beautiful avenue of beech trees, and led steeply uphill. The house stood on a plateau, from which was a glorious view of the valley below and the wooded hills beyond. The door was opened by a footman, and Kenneth entered a magnificent marble hall, filled with palms and other hothouse plants, tastefully grouped round the lovely statuary, which was of pure white marble like the portico in which it stood. A flight of marble steps led him to another door, where he was met by the butler and, conducted to the library.

Lady Earlswood welcomed him kindly, and Lady Violet, who was pouring out tea at a small table in the window, told him how delighted Evelyn was that he could come to see them. He had been obliged to make a distant call that afternoon, but would be home in a short time. Then the conversation turned on the Riviera and the happy month they had spent together there the year before, and Lady Violet went for her photo album, that she might show him the prints of the negatives which he had helped her to take. Captain Berington came in before they had looked through them all, and they talked together of the many places which the photos recalled, the different pleasant excursions during which they had been taken, and the various amusing incidents which had occurred whilst they were there. Kenneth himself appeared in several of them, and as he looked at these, he wished that he could feel once more the gay light-heartedness which he had then enjoyed.

Then it was time to dress for dinner, and he went to his room feeling as if he were in a dream, or rather, as if this were reality, and the past three weeks had been a distressing dream from which he had awaked.

He went down to the drawing-room, and found Lady Violet there before him. She looked very lovely in her pale-blue evening dress, and the magnificent diamond necklace which had been her mother's present to her when she came of age.

"I'm awfully glad you were able to come," she said in a low voice.

"Thank you, Lady Violet; I am glad too; I wanted to say good-bye to you all."

"Why good-bye?"

"May I tell you in the morning some time, if you and Lady Earlswood could spare me half an hour? I had rather not talk about it to-night, if you don't mind. I think I should like to tell you just before I go."

"But you're not going to-morrow; you must stay longer than that."

"Impossible, Lady Violet! My leave has been extended more than once, and I'm due in Aldershot to-morrow."

"Oh, what a pity! I thought—"

But what Lady Violet thought, she never told him, for at that moment her brother and sister came into the room together, and Lady Earlswood soon followed. And then dinner was announced.

The dinner-table was covered with the rarest hothouse flowers and ferns, amongst which were burning numbers of tiny electric lamps, the brightness of which was reflected in the shining silver and glass. As Kenneth Fortescue sat talking to Captain Berington after the ladies had gone into the drawing-room, he could not help wondering whether he would ever again sit down at such a table.

The evening passed pleasantly and all too quickly. Lady Earlswood had the happy gift of making all who came to her house feel at home and thoroughly at their ease, and she expressed great sorrow when Captain Fortescue announced that he must be back in Aldershot the following day.

She looked somewhat surprised when he asked her if he might speak to her on a personal matter before he started, and she glanced at Lady Violet, as if she wondered if the interview he had asked for had anything to do with her. If so, she was inclined to listen favourably to what he had to say, for

Captain Fortescue was apparently the richest man of her acquaintance, and certainly the most aristocratic in appearance. He had no title, which was, of course, a serious drawback, and she would have to make full inquiry about his family and prospects before giving her consent. But if Violet was fond of him, and if all turned out satisfactory, now that he had inherited his father's money, an offer from him would, at any rate, have her serious consideration.

Thus Lady Earlswood looked forward with anything but dissatisfaction to the appointment that she had made with Kenneth Fortescue, to come to her morning-room after breakfast the following day.

"You would like to see me alone," she whispered, as they rose from the breakfast-table and were leaving the room.

"No, Lady Earlswood; if you do not mind, I should like all of you to hear what I have to say."

Lady Earlswood was surprised. Surely his private communication could not be what she had expected. However, she at once fell in with his suggestion, and soon the family party was gathered together in her pretty boudoir.

Then he told them all; he laid before them the story of his life; he spoke tenderly of his old father, dwelling on his self-denying love in bringing him up, and educating him regardless of expense, and in such a way as to make him (he was ashamed to own it now) even feel out of place in his own home, and out of touch with his own father. He said that he had often wished to tell them of this, but a feeling of loyalty to his father had held him back from doing so.

Then he went on to the cause of his father's death; he told them of the telegram, and of the terrible news it contained; and then he spoke of the consequence of that news to himself; he said that he was on the point of throwing up his commission, inasmuch as he could not possibly live upon his captain's pay; that he must now turn his attention to something which would be sufficient to provide for him in a quiet and simple way, and which might also enable him, by means of the greatest economy, to repay an obligation incurred by his father some years ago, and for which, as his son, he felt morally responsible.

They did not interrupt him as he was telling this story, but listened attentively. Lady Violet, with heightened colour, turned a little away from him as he was speaking, and as soon as he had finished, she rose and left the room.

THEN HE TOLD THEM ALL; HE LAID BEFORE THEM THE STORY OF HIS LIFE.

THEN HE TOLD THEM ALL; HE LAID BEFORE THEM THE STORY OF HIS LIFE.

Lady Earlswood thanked him for speaking as frankly as he had done. Of course it was the only right thing to do, for, in their position of life, there were obligations which they owed to society, and her husband, the late Earl, being dead, these obligations of course devolved upon herself. She was very sorry that circumstances, over which of course he had no control, had occurred to terminate what had been a very pleasant acquaintanceship. She wished it could have been otherwise, but she felt sure he would see with her that she had no choice in the matter. At the same time she could only repeat that she was exceedingly sorry, and that she wished very much that it could have been otherwise.

It was just what Captain Fortescue had expected her to say, and he was therefore neither surprised nor disappointed. But he felt, with somewhat of a pang of regret, that he had come to the last paragraph of that last page of Volume I of his life, as he rose to take leave of her and Lady Maude.

Captain Berington, who had not spoken once during the interview, now told him that he was coming with him to the station, and would join him in a few minutes. As Kenneth passed through the inner hall on his way to the door where the carriage was waiting for him, Lady Violet was just crossing it. She was still very flushed, and he thought that she had been crying. He went up to her to say good-bye.

"I think you might have told us all this before," she said.

"I have only known it three weeks myself, Lady Violet."

"Oh! About the money—yes. But about your father—you knew that. You see, it has put us in a very unpleasant position."

"I think I explained to you why I did not tell you before; it was for my poor old father's sake."

"It makes it awfully hard for us."

"It shall not be harder than I can help, Lady Violet; you need not be afraid that I shall presume upon our former acquaintance. I know my altered position, and I shall never forget it, I hope. Good-bye."

"Good-bye, Captain Fortescue."

She did not even shake hands with him as she said it, but ran swiftly upstairs, and Kenneth passed on through the marble hall to the carriage waiting at the door.

Captain Berington was most friendly during the drive, but did not allude to the conversation that had taken place in his mother's boudoir, until he was standing at the carriage door just before the train started. Then he grasped Kenneth's hand, and said—

"You and I can still be friends, Fortescue; of course the mater has to be particular for the girls' sake, and my brother, the Earl (you've never met him, I think), is more particular still; he's obliged to be, I suppose. But I'm only a younger son, so can do as I like. Good-bye."

The train moved off before Kenneth could answer, and as it left the station behind, he felt that, in spite of Captain Berington's friendly words, he had read the very last line of the last page of Volume I of his life-story, and had come to Finis.

But as the Captain journeyed on to Aldershot, and recalled Lady Violet's words, "It makes it awfully hard for us," he could not help contrasting them with other words, spoken by another voice, only ten days before, "Please don't think about us; it is quite hard enough for you."

And, as he thought of the difference between the two remarks, he mourned less than he would otherwise have done over the Finis which he had read at the bottom of that last page.

CHAPTER X
GOOD-BYE

WHEN Louis Verner arrived at Fernbank on the morning of Captain Fortescue's departure, Marjorie was looking out for him, and as soon as he took the "Standard" out of his pocket, she ran upstairs and carried it to her own room.

Spreading the paper out on the bed, she turned to the advertisement page, and looked down the column headed "SITUATIONS VACANT." She passed quickly over those at the top of the column, "Wanted, a Gentleman of Smart Habits," "Wanted a Salesman," "Wanted a Well-educated Youth," etc., and passed on to those advertisements which referred to women.

"'A Working Housekeeper wanted for a London Business House.'

"I should not do for that," she said.

"'Lady Cook wanted at once.'

"I should not like to be a lady cook, nor do I know enough about cooking.

"Oh! This is better. 'Mother's Help—Nice young girl.' I wonder if I am a nice young girl," she said, laughing. "'Three boys, ages 11, 5, and 2. Good reference. Write fully, Mrs. Burstall, 51, Lester Street, S.E.'

"Some registry office, I suppose. I don't like the sound of that 'nice young girl.'

"Oh! Here's another. 'Mother's help wanted, fond of children, must be thoroughly domesticated, comfortable home, one servant kept. Apply by letter, Mrs. Holtby, Daisy Bank, Staffordshire.'

"That sounds better! I am fond of children. I wonder if I am thoroughly domesticated! And Daisy Bank sounds inviting. I wonder if it is the name of the house or the place. I should like to go to a pretty place, if possible. Of course it does not matter really, only after Borrowdale—" And Marjorie looked lovingly at the beautiful view from her bedroom window.

"Mother," she called, as Mrs. Douglas passed the bedroom door, "come and look at these advertisements."

Mother and daughter sat down together and read them through, and Mrs. Douglas agreed with Marjorie that the Daisy Bank one appeared to be the most promising.

"But, oh, darling," she said, "how shall I ever get on without you?"

"Or I without you, mother?" said Marjorie. "But we must do something, and this seems the best, does it not?"

"I suppose so, dear."

"And I do think it will be good for Phyllis. She is so clever and capable, when she gives her mind to anything, and I am sure she will save you all she can, and she would never settle away from home, would she?"

"Oh no, that would never do!" said Mrs. Douglas. "I don't think poor little Phyllis is cut out to rough it at all."

So that day the letter was written, and Marjorie took it herself to the post-office, and, as she dropped it into the box, felt like Julius Cæsar when he crossed the Rubicon.

How impatiently she waited for the answer! It came two days afterwards in a man's handwriting.

"COLWYN HOUSE,
"Daisy Bank.

"DEAR MISS DOUGLAS,

"Mrs. Holtby being ill and unable to write to you herself, she has asked me to inform you that we have written to your referees, and if all proves satisfactory, she will be pleased to engage you at a salary of twenty-five pounds per annum. Your duties will be quite simple, and we shall treat you as one of the family. As you ask for a reference from me, I beg to give you the following:—

"A. Crayshaw, Esq.,
"The Laurels,
"West Bromwich.

"Should you decide to come to us, we shall be pleased to receive you this day week.
"Yours truly,
"LIONEL HOLTBY."

"What do you think of it, mother?"

"I think it sounds all right, dear, but of course we must write to this Mr. Crayshaw before deciding anything."

The letter from West Bromwich proved quite satisfactory, bearing witness to the respectability of the Holtby family, and therefore, after much thought and also much prayer, Mrs. Douglas consented to Marjorie's going to Daisy Bank.

"You can come home again if all is not right," she said. "Rather than you should be unhappy, we will forfeit anything."

That last week at home seemed to fly on the wings of the wind. There was so much to be done; their heads were so fully occupied in thinking of what was needed for Marjorie's outfit, as she called it, their hands were so busy in cutting out and making sundry pretty blouses and morning dresses, that there was little time to dwell upon the parting that was coming.

It was not until the last night, when her trunk was locked and strapped and taken downstairs, and when only the dress-basket, which was to be left open until the morning, remained in her room as evidence of her coming journey, it was only then that, for a little time, Marjorie's heart failed her. It was so hard to leave them all, but especially her mother. She could not help her tears falling fast as she thought of it. She was going out into the world alone. No, not alone, her best Friend would go with her; she would not forget that. And all this had come by His ordering; it was His will that was being done. She looked up and read a card which she had bought the last time she was in Keswick, and which was hanging over her bed. In the middle of this card, in gold letters, were these two words—

"YES, LORD,"

And underneath them was this verse—

"One great eternal Yes,
 To all my Lord shall say,
To what I know, or yet shall know,
 In all the untried way."

And, as Marjorie knelt by her bed, the "Yes, Lord," was said.

When she went downstairs not a sign of trouble was left on her face. They would all feel rather dull that night, she said to herself, and she must try to cheer them.

"I wonder Marjorie can be so merry when she is going away for so long," said Phyllis that night, as she went into Leila's room to say good night to her sister.

"Marjorie never thinks of herself," was Leila's answer; "she only thinks of mother."

Phyllis stooped to kiss little Carl as he lay asleep in his cot, and as she did so, she said to herself that she would try, when Marjorie was gone, to follow in her footsteps.

The next morning was bright and frosty, and the sky was without a single cloud; the hills and dales were flooded with sunshine, which was unusually bright for the time of year. The snow had all gone, and the spring flowers were coming up fast in the garden. As Marjorie went away, she held in her hand a large bunch of violets and snowdrops, which Phyllis had gathered for her before breakfast. Her mother came with her to the gate, where Colonel Verner's dog-cart was waiting, for Louis had promised to drive her into Keswick.

It was hard work to say good-bye to her mother, but Marjorie tried to do it with a bright face; she did not want to make it harder for her mother at that moment. Then she got up beside Louis; and Phyllis, who was coming to see her off, jumped up behind.

Marjorie turned round as they drove over the bridge, and saw her mother and little Carl at the garden gate, still looking after her. She looked up at the house, and at old Dorcas, who had come to the door, and was waving her apron, and, higher still, she saw Leila, watching from the bedroom window, and she was afraid that she was crying.

Never did Borrowdale look more beautiful in Marjorie's eyes! She gazed long and lovingly at every mountain peak that came in sight; she longed to store away in her memory each bit of the loveliness, so that when she was far away she might refresh herself by the recollection of it all.

Louis was very angry that Marjorie was going from home; he would not believe that it was necessary, and he thought that when he came back for the Long Vacation, it would be a great nuisance to find her gone. He had quite come to the conclusion lately that he liked Marjorie better than Phyllis, and now she was going away from him. He wished heartily that Captain Fortescue had never come to Rosthwaite, upsetting all their plans, and making a break in the happy little party at Fernbank.

Louis Verner was good-natured and easy-going, but he had no power of taking a calm, sensible view of anything; he wanted life to go on smoothly and comfortably, and he could not see why it should not always do so.

"Louis," said Marjorie, as they drove along, "when I come home, the first question I shall ask you will be this: 'What are you going to be?' And I shall expect a satisfactory answer!"

"Oh yes. I'm sure to have decided by that time; but it's very difficult, isn't it?"

"Not if you give your mind to it, and find out what you're fit for."

"Oh yes! Well, I will try, Marjorie. It's an awful nuisance your going away; you might have helped me to settle."

"I? What nonsense, Louis! No one can do that but yourself. But you must do it. I can see Colonel Verner is very worried about it."

"Yes, I believe he is. Well, I will try. But don't let us talk about that now, Marjorie. You'll write to me, of course?"

"I will if I've time, Louis; but I don't know what my duties will be," she said, laughing.

"Oh! Never mind the duties. I shall expect to hear from you—don't forget, Marjorie."

"When do you go back to Oxford?"

"The beginning of next week; it is a grind! I feel as if I had only just come down."

They were early for the train, and walked up and down the platform till it came up. As they did so, Marjorie kept remembering many little things she wanted to say to Phyllis.

"Don't forget Leila's tea in the morning. You will get up, won't you?"

"Oh yes, Marjorie."

"And look after mother, and if she seems tired, get her to rest a little. And, Phyllis, do be careful that Carl doesn't go near the river; that garden gate ought always to be kept shut."

Then the engine came steaming into the station with the Cockermouth train behind it, and in a few minutes Marjorie was leaning out of the window and waving a last good-bye to Louis and Phyllis, who had run to the end of the platform to watch the train out of sight.

CHAPTER XI
DAISY BANK

IT was quite dark that evening when Marjorie drew near her journey's end. She had to change at Wolverhampton and to go to another station, that she might travel by the Great Western line.

"What time do I get to Daisy Bank?" she asked the porter who put her box into the van.

"In ten minutes, miss; third station."

She was alone in the carriage, and she sat looking out of the window, and wondering what she would find when she reached her destination. She noticed a bright light in the sky, and after a minute or two she saw that it came from the furnaces of several large ironworks that she was passing. By their bright light she could see the men at work, their faces lighted up by the red glow. But all this time she was carefully counting the stations. One passed; two passed. She must get out at the next.

The train stopped. She could hear the porter shouting, "Dysy Bank, Dysy Bank," with true Staffordshire pronunciation. She got out of the carriage, wondering who would be there to meet her. At first she could see no one; but, as she walked along the platform to get her luggage out of the van, a girl of about twelve years came up to her.

"Are you Miss Douglas?"

"Yes, I am. Have you come to meet me?"

"Yes. You're to leave your box at the station, and father will send for it."

"Can't I get a cab?"

The girl laughed. "Cab!" she said. "I should think not! We've no cabs here."

They left the box in the care of the porter, and the girl led the way to a steep flight of stone steps leading to the road above. Then she went along a roughly made cinder-path, and Marjorie followed a little behind, at times plunging into great pools of water which she could not see in the dim light, and at other times almost falling on the slippery mud. Then they turned into a short street, if street it could be called. It was so irregular that it seemed to Marjorie as if houses of all kinds had been thrown down there, and left to find their own level and own position. They passed one or two squalid shops, which appeared to sell little besides shrivelled oranges and the commonest of cheap sweets.

As they went under the light of one of these, Marjorie glanced at her companion. She was a tall, thin girl, with sharp features and an utterly colourless face. Her hair, which lacked colour almost as much as her face, being of that light yellow ochre tint which has the appearance of having been soaked in soda and water to bleach it; it was untidily done, and hung loosely about her face. She was wearing a brown tam-o'-shanter and a long grey coat, two buttons of which were missing. There was a knowing, womanly look about her face, as if she had never been a child, but had begun life as a grown-up person.

As they walked on together, the street lamps became fewer, with long stretches of darkness between them, and at length the furnace lights formed the only illumination, and these every here and there revealed a scene of utter desolation.

"What a curious place!" Marjorie said to the girl at her side.

"I should just think it is," she answered. "I hate it, and mother does too!"

"Why do you live here, then?"

"Oh! Father is the manager at the works over there. We have to live here, I suppose; it's a hateful place!"

"What is your name?"

"Patty. Did you ever hear such an awful name? I detest it. I can't think how ever they brought themselves to give me a name like that. It's the name of father's aunt, worse luck, and she asked him to call me after her."

"How many are there of you?"

"Seven; isn't it a lot? I wish we weren't such a crowd."

"Are you all at home?"

"Yes. We go to school, of course."

"Then there is a school here."

"Oh yes, a big one. I'm very glad you've come, Miss Douglas."

"Thank you; it's nice to have a welcome."

"You see, we're all so upset since mother got so ill; she's almost always in bed now. She hasn't been up for five weeks at all, and we do get in a muddle. I do what I can, but I can't do much. I have to go to school, you see, and our girl is so slow. She's not a bad sort, but she can't hurry; some people can't. And the boys are so tiresome, and they won't do what I tell them."

"Where are we going now?" asked Marjorie, as they seemed to be leaving the road and turning into the darkness.

"Oh, it's a short cut over the mounds. Take hold of my arm; you can't see, and you'll be walking off into one of the pit-pools. The lakes we call them," she added, with a laugh. "You come from the Lakes, don't you?"

"Yes, from such a lovely place."

"Well, you won't like our lakes, I'm afraid. They're only rainwater that lies in the hollows between the mounds. There are plenty of them about here."

"Isn't it better to keep to the road such a dark night as this?"

"You can't," said Patty, "it's all deep mud; you'd stick fast if you tried."

At length they saw a light, which came from the windows of a square stone house with a small garden in front of it, and Patty took a latchkey from her pocket and opened the door. Immediately a rush was heard from an inner room, and six children of various ages ran out to see the newcomer.

"Shake hands properly, and don't stand staring," said Patty. "Tom and Walter, Miss Douglas; they come next to me. Then there are Nellie and Alice. Oh! Alice, what a dirty pinafore you have. Why didn't you get Bessie to put you a clean one on? And here are the two babies. Come and kiss Miss Douglas, Bob and Evie. They're very dirty; they almost always are dirty, but they're such darlings!"

"How old are they?" asked Marjorie, as she stooped to kiss the cleanest part of the dirty little cheeks.

"Just three; they're twins, you know. Now run away, children; Miss Douglas must come and see mother."

She spoke as though they were all many years younger than herself, and as if all the cares of the household rested on her shoulders. Marjorie followed her upstairs, and she led the way into a bedroom where Mrs. Holtby was lying in bed.

Marjorie thought it was one of the most untidy rooms she had ever seen. Dust lay upon everything, and the table, chest of drawers, bed and floor were covered with all manner of things, crowded together in hopeless confusion. Mrs. Holtby raised herself on her pillow as Marjorie came in.

"I'm glad to see you, Miss Douglas. Oh! What beautiful violets."

Marjorie at once took them out of her coat and gave them to her.

"Oh! How delicious; they remind me of home."

"Did you live in the country?"

"Yes, all my life, till I was married, Miss Douglas. I'm afraid you won't find things very comfortable, but I can't help it."

"No, of course you can't," said Marjorie, kindly.

"Patty has got your room ready, haven't you, Patty?"

"Yes, as well as I could," said the girl; "I'm afraid it isn't very nice."

"Never mind," said Marjorie, "we'll soon get all straight. May I take my things off?"

Patty led the way to a small back bedroom, rather scantily furnished, but, unlike the one she had just left, it was tidy and fairly clean. She was surprised to see a little bunch of ivy lying on the dressing-table.

"Who put this here?" she asked.

"I did," said Patty. "It isn't black; I washed it at the tap. I thought as you came from the country you'd like to see something green."

Marjorie turned round and gave her a kiss.

"Thank you, dear," she said. "I do like it very much."

But, in spite of this kindly thought on Patty's part, it was hard for Marjorie to resist the feeling of home-sickness which crept over her when she was left alone. How could she ever live in such surroundings, so utterly different from everything to which she had been accustomed? But she determined to be brave and hopeful, and went downstairs to find tea ready for her in the dining-room. The cloth was dirty and the food not tempting, but Patty, who poured out the tea, seemed so ashamed of it all, and so anxious that she should have what she wanted, that she felt obliged to eat as much as she could, lest she should be disappointed.

After tea Mr. Holtby came in, a tall silent man, with sandy hair and a most worried expression on his face.

"Glad to see you, Miss Douglas. I hope Patty has taken care of you. Patty, I want some stamps. Just put on your hat and get some."

Without a word Patty set out in the darkness, and soon returned with what he wanted.

"Patty, those boys are quarrelling in the next room; go and see what's the matter," said her father.

"I expect Patty is tired," said Marjorie; "I'll go."

The boys stopped quarrelling when Marjorie entered, and a packet of chocolates which she brought from her pocket soon restored harmony in the back sitting-room, as it was called. She then went up to Mrs. Holtby, that she might learn what she wanted her to do.

Marjorie found that Mrs. Holtby was superior in many ways to her husband, a gentle, kindhearted woman, but borne down by ill-health and the cares of her large family. Her father had been a land-agent, and she had lived in a lonely place in Shropshire, and had known far better days. Marjorie felt sorry for her and anxious to help her.

But it was late when she got to bed that night, and she felt almost as if life in that house would be more than she could bear. And then she remembered that she had come there willing to do God's will, whatever that might be, and she determined to make the best of the home to which she had come, and to do her utmost to brighten it.

The next morning Marjorie was awakened at six o'clock by the "bulls" in the different works calling the men to begin their labour for the day. She jumped up, wondering what the noise was and where she could be. Then she remembered to what a forlorn place she had come the night before, and she determined to make things a little more comfortable as soon as possible. She lighted the gas and dressed quickly, and as she was doing so, she heard Mr. Holtby knocking at the servant's door and telling her to get up.

Marjorie was downstairs long before the maid, and finding a little gas-stove in the back kitchen, she lighted it and boiled some water in a small kettle which was standing on the shelf. Mrs. Holtby was very much surprised when, as soon as her husband had gone downstairs, there came a knock at her door, and Marjorie entered with a cup of tea and a thin slice of bread and butter.

"Oh! How nice," she said. "I am so thirsty; I have had such a restless night. Whatever made you think of it?"

"I have an invalid sister at home," Marjorie said, "so you see, I know what invalids like. Now I will help Bessie to get breakfast ready, and then dress the babies."

The next hour and a half was a very busy time. It was like starting a regiment, to get all those children off to school. Everything that they wanted was lost, and the scampering up and downstairs after books, boots, hats, caps, and coats was a most wearying proceeding.

At last they were off, and the house was quiet; only the two babies were left behind, and they were busily playing on the floor with a large box of bricks. Then Marjorie went upstairs to take Mrs. Holtby's breakfast, and to see what she could do to make her comfortable. She felt that nothing short of a regular spring cleaning of the bedroom would make it really clean and as she longed to see it, but she did not like to propose that the first day. She must get Bessie to help her, if that was to be done, and Bessie could not be driven too fast. She had her own ideas, and these were conservative to the last degree.

So on this first morning, Marjorie contented herself with smaller measures of reform. She brought warm water and sponged the sick woman's face and hands, and then she went quietly about the room, tidying it and clearing away the piles of rubbish which it contained. The children's clothes she carried to their own room, the books and papers she dusted and took downstairs, and then, after shaking up the pillows and straightening the bed clothes, she went downstairs to see what Bessie was doing about dinner.

"What time do they come in, Bessie?"

"One o'clock, and the master a quarter past."

"What is there for dinner?"

"There's a piece of beef; I can cook that."

"That's right, Bessie. What about pudding?"

"Well, we haven't had many puddings lately, not since missus has been ill."

"Do you think I should make one, Bessie?"

"Yes, if you will. They won't half smile if you do."

This, Marjorie discovered, was the Daisy Bank way of expressing great satisfaction.

"Very well, Bessie; let me see what you have in the house."

Marjorie was a good cook, and soon made a large suet pudding with plenty of raisins in it for the children, and a dainty custard pudding for their mother. Then she laid the table for dinner, for which she found a clean table-cloth, washed and polished the electro-plated forks and spoons, made the dull and dirty tumblers shine brightly, by washing them first in hot and then in cold water, and afterwards rubbing them with a dry cloth, and managed to have the dinner cooked and all in readiness by the time that the boys and girls came in from school.

"You have made it nice, Miss Douglas," Patty said as she looked at the table; "I wish mother could see it."

"Will you help me to get mother's dinner ready, Patty?"

"Yes. What shall I do?"

"Find me a little tray; and, Patty, have you any serviettes?"

"Yes, there are some in a drawer upstairs; I'll get one."

Patty was only too delighted to help, and when Mrs. Holtby's dinner was ready, carried the tray with great glee up to the sick room.

Mr. Holtby looked round with satisfaction as he took his place at the head of the table, but he said nothing. He was a most silent man, and Marjorie found that his words of commendation were at all times few and far between.

That afternoon Mrs. Holtby insisted on Marjorie's going out for an hour or two, that she might get some fresh air after her hard work. She proposed taking the twins with her, but their mother said that the roads were too wet for their thin shoes, and that they would be quite happy playing in her room; so she set out alone, not sorry to feel free for a little time.

So far Marjorie had seen practically nothing of Daisy Bank, for it was too dark the night before for her to do more than see the dim outline of what she passed, and from the windows of Colwyn House there was merely a narrow view, shut in by houses on either side. She had not expected to see much to charm her during her walk, but she was hardly prepared for the scene of utter desolation that met her eyes as she went down the muddy lane leading from the house.

On one side of it were a few tumble-down cottages, damp and discoloured; on the other was an open waste, strewn with the remains of old furnace heaps. She looked across this wilderness to the huge pit mounds, rising in all directions, the very picture of gloom and dreariness.

Finding that the lane was still impassable from the depth of mud, she turned upon the waste common, parts of which were covered with thin, smoke-begrimed grass. Here there stood two old houses, even more wretched and forlorn than those she had already passed. The bedroom window of one was partly blocked with wood, and the room was given up to pigeons, which flew in and out at pleasure. The door of the other house was open, and she saw a cock and a hen and three fat ducks walking about as if the whole place belonged to them.

Further on she came upon two ragged women, down on their knees upon an old mound, raking over the muddy ashes, and picking out the wet and dirty cinders which were to be found amongst them, and then stowing them away in an old sack.

"What are you doing?" Marjorie asked.

"Getting cinders for the fire."

"Will they burn?" she asked in astonishment.

"Yes, with a little coal. It's better than no fire at all."

Marjorie walked on, sick at heart, as she thought of the kind of homes that those women must have. The cold, icy wind was blowing in her face, and she shivered as she thought of the apology for a fire which would be kindled with those lifeless cinders.

After this she passed more houses and more mounds; but nowhere in the whole place did she see a vestige of anything whatever that was pleasant to look upon. The houses were destitute of paint, the doors and window-frames were bare and unsightly, the numberless broken panes were filled in with rag or paper. More than one of the houses was in ruins—every window broken, and the walls ready to fall in. The mines below had caused these houses to sink; they had been pronounced unsafe, and had been left deserted, but no one had taken the trouble to clear away the ugly, dismal ruins. There they stood, blackened with furnace smoke, unsightly and melancholy objects.

Only two coal-pits were working, so a man told her, who was smoking a dirty clay pipe at his door. Some had stopped because of bad trade; some were worked out; some had filled with water, and were therefore abandoned. Yet at the mouth of each of these deserted pits, the heavy wooden frame and great wheel still remained—a gloomy memento of more prosperous days.

In every direction in which she looked, Marjorie saw unmistakable marks of squalid, cheerless poverty; the only prosperous-looking building being the public-house at the corner, which appeared to do a thriving trade. The whole country was honeycombed with mines, and, in consequence, many of the houses had sunk below the level of the others in the same row. Everything in Daisy Bank seemed crooked and out of shape. Other cottages were scattered amongst the furnace débris, were built anywhere and everywhere that a place could be found for them, on different levels and in sundry nooks and corners of the hilly waste.

Then she came to higher mounds still, and crossing these she saw deep, black pools in their hollows, stretches of dark, stagnant water, which never reflected anything that was pretty or bright except the moon in God's pure heaven above. Here and there some one, more thrifty than his neighbours, had made a little garden in the waste; but what could grow in such a smoky atmosphere and in such poor and barren soil? A few struggling plants of the most hardy kinds were all that the best garden in Daisy Bank could produce.

Marjorie was glad to get back even to the dismal house in which her lot was cast; it seemed almost cheerful to her after the unkempt hideousness of its depressing surroundings.

CHAPTER XII
BLACK COUNTRY ROSES

THAT first day at Daisy Bank was a fair sample of many others which followed it. Bit by bit order was restored to the once untidy and comfortless house. Mrs. Holtby's room was made as sweet and cheerful as it was possible for any room in such a neighbourhood to be; the floor was washed, the carpet shaken, clean white curtains were hung in the window, and fresh hangings on the bed; whilst upon the table stood a vase, which was filled with spring flowers, a constant supply of which was sent regularly by Phyllis from the dear home garden.

Then Marjorie took another room in hand, and, with Bessie's and Patty's help, worked the same reformation there, and so by degrees the house looked more home-like and far less dreary. But it was a hard life to which she had come, and sometimes she felt inclined to despair.

Work as hard as she might, from early in the morning till late at night, she could never keep pace with the darning and patching, the clearing and dusting, which seemed always waiting to be done. Her feet were weary with running up and down stairs; her head ached with the noise of the children, and at times she longed terribly for a single day's holiday and rest; but of this she saw no prospect whatever. Beyond a daily run over the pit mounds, she never got out, and she saw no one in these walks to whom she could speak. Her thoughts were her only companions, and they were anxious ones at times.

The home letters sounded bright, as a rule, but now and again some sentence in her mother's made her feel how much she was missed there. Her own letters were as cheerful as she could make them, although she wrote a truthful account of the place to which she had come, for she had promised her mother that she would do so.

As Marjorie wandered over the wilderness of ashes day after day, she thought of them all and of her pretty home, and a terrible yearning came over her to see them again, and to look even for five minutes at the scenes she loved so well. And then her thoughts would wander to Captain Fortescue. She had kept her promise to him before leaving home; she had written to tell him where she was going, but she had never received an answer; sometimes she wondered whether her letter had ever reached him. What was he doing now? Had he left the army? Was he happy la the new life upon which she supposed he must have entered? She thought of his words to her mother,—

"I shall allow myself in no luxury until all is paid."

What a hard life that would mean, if he kept his word! And she believed that he would keep his word; she felt that he was a man to be trusted. Over and over again her busy thoughts returned to this subject, and in her prayers for those at home, his name was added. It could not be wrong to pray for him, surely.

One day when spring weather was beginning, and when even Daisy Bank looked a degree less dismal, Marjorie found a friend. As she passed one of the tumble-down cottages, she noticed an old man who was coming out of it with a rose-tree in his arms, and then she saw that a row of similar pots stood in the sunshine against the discoloured wall of the house. The roses were just coming into leaf, and she noticed that the old man was bending lovingly over them, loosening the soil near their stems, and giving each of them some water from a jug which was standing on the doorstep. Marjorie felt that at last she had found something in Daisy Bank at which it was pleasant to look. She went up to the old man and admired his roses, and he showed them to her with great pride, telling her the name and the colour of each.

"Would you like to see my garden, miss?" he asked.

He took her through the kitchen, which was quite clean, although bare of paint and whitewash, and led her to the back of his cottage. There he showed her his lawn, a tiny strip of green about three feet long and two feet broad, covered with grass. This he watered daily, to keep it from being blackened by the smoke-laden atmosphere, and kept it short by cutting it every evening with a pair of scissors. He was intensely proud of it, however, and of a row of hardy plants which were leading a struggling existence under the wall of the house. London Pride was, perhaps, the only one which did not appear to be depressed by its surroundings, and which might justly have changed its name to Daisy Bank Pride.

But the old man was proud of them all, and beamed with delight when Marjorie stooped to examine them. That tiny garden was the joy of his heart, as dear to him as the lovely home garden had been to her, and quite as beautiful in his eyes.

"It's a wonder that anything will grow here," she said.

"Ay, it's unlikely soil; but the Lord's plants do thrive sometimes in that."

"Yes," said Marjorie, for she did not quite see what he meant.

"There was old Dan'el in Babylon, and Obadiah, him as lived in Jezebel's time, and there was saints in Nero's household. They had bad soil, all of 'em, but they was faithful 'trees of the Lord's planting,' that He might be glorified."

And then Marjorie felt that she had found a friend. Old Enoch would have been stamped as an ignorant man by many, but he knew his Bible well, and could repeat much of it by heart. It was his daily study, and he was taught by the Spirit of God. Many and many a time, when things seemed darker than usual, Marjorie would run in to see him, and she always came away feeling brighter and better.

It was on the very day upon which she first made old Enoch's acquaintance that, as she was going back to Colwyn House, she had a great and most unexpected surprise. Coming along the lane to meet her, and picking his way amongst the pools which even the spring sunshine had not dried up, she saw a well-known figure, and her heart danced with joy at the sight, for it seemed to her like a bit of home put down amongst the dreariness of Daisy Bank.

It was Louis Verner!

"Oh, Louis, how nice to see you!" she cried. "It is lovely to see a home face!"

"I thought you would be pleased to see me, Marjorie. I'm on my way home, and I thought I could tell them about you."

"And you've come out of your way on purpose to see me! How awfully good of you, Louis!"

"Not at all good; I wanted to come. Marjorie, you're prettier than ever!"

"Don't talk such nonsense, Louis!" she said. "Tell me about yourself. How have you been getting on?"

"Oh, fairly well, I think. We've had an awfully jolly term; all sorts of things going on."

"And what are you going to be?"

"Now, Marjorie, that's too bad! You said you would ask me when you came home next."

"Very well, I won't scold you to-day, when you've been so good as to come and see me. How long can you stay?"

"Only an hour."

"Will you come in?"

"I'd rather not," said Louis; "we can't talk if all those people are there. Can't you come for a walk?"

"I'll ask Mrs. Holtby."

The permission was readily given; and Mrs. Holtby, who was sitting up in her room, crept to the window, and peeped through the blind with true feminine curiosity, to see who was the friend from home with whom her much-valued mother's help was so anxious to go out.

"A very particular friend, I should imagine," she said to herself with a smile, as the two disappeared together over the pit mounds.

"Marjorie," said Louis, as she joined him, "of all detestable and hateful places on the face of this earth, I do think Daisy Bank is the worst!"

"Don't be too hard on it, Louis! You should see it at night, when the sky is lit up by the furnace lights. We have constant illuminations here."

"I don't know what Mrs. Douglas will say when I tell her."

"Then you mustn't tell her, Louis. I shall be very angry if you make it out blacker than it is."

"I couldn't do that," said Louis, laughing, "if I were to try."

"Well, what does it matter, Louis? If I don't mind it, why should anybody else?"

They came now to one of the large dark pools.

"What a ghastly hole!" he said. "Just the place to tempt a fellow to commit suicide."

"Now, Louis! That is our best lake, the Derwentwater of these parts."

"Derwentwater, indeed!" said Louis, scornfully. "Look here, Marjorie! I don't like your being here at all."

"I assure you, Louis, there is no need to pity me."

Then Louis suddenly changed his tone.

"Marjorie."

"Yes, Louis."

"Why do you never write to me?"

"I haven't time, Louis; it's as much as I can do to write home."

"But I do think you might write to me, because I am—well, I really am awfully fond of you, Marjorie. Do you know I like you better than any girl I know? Upon my word I do."

"Thank you, Louis," said Marjorie, with a mock bow, "that's a very pretty compliment."

"It isn't a compliment, Marjorie; at least I mean it's quite a true one. Did you get the picture postcards I sent you?"

"Yes, thank you, Louis; I asked mother, if she was writing to you, to thank you for them."

"So she did; but I had rather have had a letter from you, Marjorie."

They were walking towards the railway station when the hour was over, and Louis's train was almost due, when he said suddenly—

"Marjorie, I'm going away, and you haven't said anything nice to me."

"Now that isn't a compliment!" she said, laughing again. "Look, Louis! The signal is down; we must hurry."

They ran down the steps, and he had barely time to get his ticket before the train came in.

As he jumped into the carriage, Marjorie could not help wishing that she was going with him, or at any rate that she was on her way to the same destination.

CHAPTER XIII
MOTHER HOTCHKISS

As time went on, in spite of her hard work, Marjorie began to feel not merely accustomed to the life at Colwyn House, but really fond of the people with whom she lived. Mrs. Holtby was very grateful for all that she had done for them, and was willing to fall in with any suggestion that she might make. Her health was gradually returning, and she was able to come downstairs, and to relieve Marjorie of several lighter duties.

As for Patty, she was Marjorie's firm ally and most willing helper, and Marjorie rejoiced when she saw the look of care departing from the child's face, as she realized that the burden of the family no longer rested upon her shoulders. The boys were at times exceedingly naughty and troublesome, but the little ones were devoted to "Miss Duggie" as they called her, and loved to sit on her knee listening to Bible stories, or to children's hymns which she sang to them. Their mother would often creep into the room and listen too; she told Marjorie that it made her think of her own mother, and of the lessons she had learnt long ago, but which, alas she feared that she had forgotten.

On Sunday Marjorie took the elder ones to the church, which stood on a hill overlooking the cindery waste, and which could be seen from any part of its forlorn parish. Mr. Holtby never went to any place of worship; both he and his wife had fallen into careless ways, and had become accustomed, after years of neglect, to regard Sunday as little more than an excuse for a better dinner than usual, and an opportunity for a certain amount of self-indulgence.

One day in the early summer, when the sun was shining as brightly in Daisy Bank as in more favoured spots, Marjorie was standing at old Enoch's door, once more admiring his roses. They were actually coming into bud, and the old man's excitement was great as he counted the coming blossoms.

"The very first that comes out shall be for you, Miss Douglas."

"Thank you, Enoch; I wonder which it will be."

"This Crimson Rambler, Miss, I believe. Look at it; you can just see the colour coming in the bud."

"So I can!"

"Miss Douglas," the old man went on, "do you ever go to see old Mother Hotchkiss?"

"What a name! No, I never heard of her."

"She lives in that old house down the lane; you must have noticed it, surely; two big square windows, almost like shop windows, and lots of nice plants in them."

"Oh yes, I know."

"Well, I wish you'd go and see her; I don't think she's long for this world, and she's as ignorant as a heathen in Africa."

"Poor old thing!"

"Ay! You may well say, 'Poor old thing!' Miss Douglas, she knows nothing. She can neither read nor write, and as for Scripture, why, a baby in yon schools over there knows more about it."

"I'll go and see her, Enoch. Who looks after her?"

"Nobody much; the neighbours go in a bit, and I do what I can."

"Has she no one belonging to her?"

"She has a daughter, but she's married and away—a pretty girl too. She went to this school, and she was a good hand at learning, so I believe; they made her a pupil teacher, and her mother wasn't half proud of her. But she went to be a teacher up in the North-country somewhere, and she got married there, and now I'm told that her and her husband have gone abroad—and except Carrie, I don't believe poor old Mother Hotchkiss has anybody else belonging to her."

"It's a funny name," said Marjorie.

"You're right there, Miss; it's a gipsy name. There are a lot of Hotchkisses about here; there's one street in Wolverhampton full of them. This old body has gipsy blood in her, if I'm not mistaken; she looks like it, anyhow."

The next day Marjorie fulfilled her promise to Enoch, and knocked at the door of the house in the lane. The old woman came to open it, with a red shawl over her head.

"Mrs. Hotchkiss," said Marjorie, "I've brought you a few flowers that came this morning from my home in the country."

"Are they for me?" said the old woman, stretching out her hand eagerly for the moss rosebuds and mignonette. "Come in, Miss. I've seen you pass; you're Holtby's girl, arn't you?"

"Yes," said Marjorie, smiling to herself at her new name, "and Enoch told me you were not well."

"I'm very ill, Miss—awful bad, getting worse every day, that's what I am."

Marjorie followed her through a large room with wooden beams across the ceiling, and entered an inner room, larger still.

"What a large house you have, Mrs. Hotchkiss!"

"Too large!" groaned the old woman. "It used to be a farm."

"A farm here!" exclaimed Marjorie.

"Yes, long ago, in the old time when they hadn't found the coal; it was all country here then."

"It looks like a very old house," said Marjorie, as she noticed the overhanging chimney-piece with its long, narrow shelf, on which stood a china tea-pot and various other treasures. On either side of it was a deep recess or chimney corner, in which were curious, ancient cupboards, only about two feet in height, and having dark oaken doors. Opening out of this large kitchen was a stone flight of steps, leading down to an underground dairy, with three wide shelves one above another. These, in the olden time, were kept spotlessly clean, and were covered with large flat bowls of milk and cream; but now they were thickly coated with dirt, and were piled with all manner of rubbish.

The old woman could not talk for some time, for the effort of going to the door had brought on a severe fit of coughing, so, whilst she recovered her breath, Marjorie had plenty of time to look round the room. It was frightfully untidy and dirty, but that did not surprise her, for old Mrs. Hotchkiss was too ill to do more than creep out of bed and come downstairs to the fire, where she sat in an old armchair with her feet on the fender.

"Have you been ill long?" she asked, when the old woman was able to speak.

"Ever since Carrie went away. Not so bad as this, though. I'm getting worse every day."

"May I come and see you sometimes?"

"Yes, my dear, do."

"Would you like me to read to you a little when I come?"

"Ay, do; I can't read. There was none of this schooling in my day, and it's lonesome sitting here and doing nothing."

"Then I'll come to-morrow. I always get out about this time, and I'll come as often as I can."

When Marjorie left old Mother Hotchkiss she looked at her watch, and saw that it was time that she was going home, as it was getting near teatime.

But, as soon as she opened the door of Colwyn House, Bessie, who was cleaning the kitchen, left her work and came to meet her. "There's a gentleman been here while you were gone, Miss. He didn't look half sorry when I said you was out. He said he would look if he could see you about anywheres."

"Who was he?"

"He didn't leave any name. He was an awful nice gentleman, too!"

"Bessie, could you see that Mrs. Holtby gets her tea, if I go to look for him?"

"Yes; I'll see to her."

Marjorie said to herself that Louis would be so disappointed if he missed her, after again coming so far out of his way to see her.

"Which way did he go, Bessie?"

"Well, I told him I thought you had gone Bradley way, so I should think you'd find him somewhere over there. He hasn't been gone long."

Marjorie hurried on over the muddy road, and then climbed one of the highest mounds, that she might be able to see in which direction Louis had gone. Yes, there he was, crossing the opposite one, and coming to meet her.

But no; it was not Louis! Her heart beat quickly as she saw who it was. It was Captain Fortescue!

"Miss Douglas! I've found you at last!"

"I am so sorry you have had such a hunt. Where have you come from, Captain Fortescue?"

"Not Captain Fortescue," he said. "I have dropped that title since I left the army. I am living in Birmingham now."

"Oh! So near as that? I mean I did not know you were anywhere in this neighbourhood," she explained.

"Yes; I have been in Birmingham a fortnight now. Thank you for keeping your promise, Miss Douglas."

"Oh! Then you did get my letter?"

"Yes, I did. I meant to answer it when I could tell you what I was going to do, and then I found that Birmingham was to be my headquarters, so I thought I would come and answer it by word of mouth."

"What are you doing in Birmingham?"

"I'm an agent for a large insurance company. I think I'm very fortunate to get anything to do so soon—it's a pretty good appointment, too. I hope each quarter to be able to send a small instalment to Rosthwaite, Miss Douglas."

"It is very good of you," she answered; "but I do hope you are not stinting yourself by doing so. It troubles me very much when I think that you are."

He gave her a pleased, grateful look as she said this.

"Now, Miss Douglas, you are never to trouble about me again. I have given up smoking, and one or two little things that I am all the better without, but, beyond that, I assure you I am not straitened in any way. How could I take a nice holiday like this, if I were short of money?"

"I'm afraid it is not a very pleasant place for you to come to for a holiday," she said, laughing.

"It doesn't quite come up to our last walk together."

"Where was that? Oh, I remember. Up to Seatoller and Honister. How far away it all seems!"

"How is old Mary? How does she get on without you?"

"Oh! Poor old thing. Mother goes to see her when she can. I've just found an old woman here, Captain Fortescue."

"Have you? Is she like old Mary?"

"Oh dear no! A poor dirty old woman, half a gipsy, I think; but I'm glad to have some one to go and see."

They were standing now beside one of the dismal ponds, in which a number of ragged boys were wading.

"Miss Douglas," he said, "I am going to ask you a question, and I want a truthful answer. I know you will give me one."

"How awfully solemn it sounds!" she said, laughing. "Nothing very dreadful, I hope?"

"No, not dreadful, but something I want very much to know. Are you happy here?"

"Oh yes!" Marjorie said. "I think I can truthfully say that I am. Of course it is a very busy life; but I'm getting fond of the people, and it is far better than I expected it would be."

"Thank you," he said. "Now I wonder if you would mind doing something else for me?"

"I will if I can, Captain Fortescue."

"Will you tell me exactly what your life here is? Take an ordinary day, yesterday, for instance. Tell me what time you got up and went to bed, and give me a sketch of the day."

She did as he asked her, in as lively and cheerful a way as she could, making the best of everything, and dwelling very little on the discomforts of her life, or on the hard work which she had to do.

"Thank you," he said again, when she had finished. "I'm afraid you will think me awfully inquisitive, but I had a reason for wishing to know."

"A reason, did you say? What was it?"

He hesitated a little before answering her.

"Never mind," she said. "Don't tell me, if you had rather not."

"Oh, I don't mind your knowing, if you don't mind my telling you, Miss Douglas. You see, I sometimes—I often think of you, and wonder what you are doing—and now I shall be able to picture it out."

They walked on without speaking for a minute or two after that, and then he looked at his watch and said he must catch the next train at Deepfields, as that was the best way to get back to Birmingham, and as the station was some way off he would have to go in that direction.

"What a long way for you to go back!" he said suddenly. "Don't come any farther."

"Do let me come," she said. "I so seldom have any one to talk to."

They spoke of many things after that, and the time seemed to fly all too quickly.

"I have enjoyed my holiday very much," he said, as they stood on the platform waiting for the train. "May I give you my card? That is my address in Birmingham. Now, you made me a promise when we said good-bye last, and I want you to make me another promise now."

"What is it?" she asked.

"It is this; that if you are in any difficulty or trouble, if things don't go happily in any way, you will write to me or come to me. Will you promise?"

"Yes, I will."

"Thank you. Good-bye."

He jumped into the train as he said this, and she stood watching on the platform till it was out of sight.

CHAPTER XIV
THE OLD OAK CUPBOARD

THE year was passing on; day after day, week after week, month after month, following each other in quick succession, and Marjorie was keeping a private calendar of her own, and counting the days that must still pass before Christmas came, when she was to go home for her first holiday.

Daisy Bank did not alter much with the changing seasons: there was very little to mark the progression of spring, summer, and autumn. Barely a tree was in sight, and the few that were to be found were so stunted, blighted, and covered with smoke that the spring freshness of their leaves lasted but a few days. Upon the mounds grew a few coarse daisies—at least, the children called them daisies; they were a kind of feverfew with a daisy-like flower. Nothing else would grow there, which is perhaps why the place got its name, a name which had at first appeared to Marjorie to be utterly unsuitable.

During all the summer months and throughout the early autumn, her life had been most uneventful and monotonous. There was the daily routine of household duties, "the common round, the daily task," but nothing more. No one else came to see her, and from that day in June, when he had stepped into the Birmingham train, she had seen and heard nothing more of Captain Fortescue. She always thought of him by his old name, even though she knew that he had dropped the title.

The arrival of the home letters was the great event of Marjorie's week, and she read and re-read them until she almost knew them by heart. They made her home-sick at times, but she fought bravely against the feeling, and looked on hopefully to Christmas.

All this time, old Mrs. Hotchkiss had been growing more and more feeble, and as autumn advanced, she was quite unable to leave her bed. A rough girl of sixteen, who lived next door, waited upon her, and she seemed to have plenty of money to pay her, and she was never behind-hand in her rent. How she lived, Enoch did not know; he told Marjorie that she used to be very badly off, and that he had often seen her scraping up the cinders on the ash-heaps, but he fancied that now Carrie must be sending her money, as she seemed to have sufficient for all she wanted. Marjorie often took her soup, and milk puddings, which Mrs. Holtby was pleased that she should make for her, and she was always grateful for these. She much enjoyed hearing Marjorie read, and a feeble glimmer of light seemed to have penetrated to her poor dark soul.

But one day, late in October, when Marjorie went to see her, she found the old woman crying and evidently in great trouble.

"What is it, Mother Hotchkiss?"

"The doctor has been," she said, "and he says as how I won't be long now. I heard him tell Anna Maria when she let him out."

"Well, don't cry," said Marjorie; "you know what I told you when I was here last."

"Yes, I think of it all the time."

"And have you said that little prayer?"

"Yes, I have;

 "'O Lord, forgive me my sins, for Jesus Christ's sake.'

"I've said it scores of times; but I don't believe He will forgive me, all the same."

"Why not?"

"Oh! Because—because! But I mustn't tell you. You see, I promised not to tell; but He'll never forgive me, I know He won't."

"But He says He will. 'If we confess our sins, He is faithful and just to forgive us our sins.'"

"Yes, that's just it; that's just what I mean, my dear. If we confess our sins; but I haven't confessed my sin. See?"

"But, dear Mother Hotchkiss, you must confess it," said Marjorie.

"But I can't—I can't—you don't understand, my dear. It's something as I can't confess."

Marjorie talked to her for some time longer, and the old woman cried very much, and said again and again that she wanted to tell her, but she couldn't, no, she couldn't. At last Marjorie was obliged to leave her; she felt very sorry for her, and when she knelt to pray before getting into bed, she prayed very earnestly for the poor ignorant old woman who was so fast passing away, that she might find comfort and peace before the end came.

Marjorie was tired that night, and soon fell asleep. She was dreaming that she was in Borrowdale, sitting on a stone by the river, when suddenly a pebble hit the rock on which she was perched, and she looked up to see Louis's merry face on the bank above her. Then another pebble came, and she woke. No, she was not in Borrowdale, but in her little bedroom in Daisy Bank. What was that noise, then? Some one was throwing pebbles at her window! She was very much startled, but got out of bed and looked out. It was quite dark, and she could see no one. She opened her window a little way and said, "Who is there?"

"It's me, Miss," said old Enoch's voice. "Poor Mother Hotchkiss is much worse, and she wouldn't give us any peace till we said we would fetch you. She says she must see you, and she can't die happy till she has."

"Who is with her, Enoch?"

"Peggy Jones, that's Anna Maria's mother; but I've been there the last hour. They fetched me. See?"

"I'll come, Enoch."

"I'll wait for you, Miss, and take you across," he said.

Marjorie dressed quickly, and knocking at Mr. and Mrs. Holtby's door, she explained where she was going and why. Mr. Holtby got up and let her out, and then, guided through the darkness by old Enoch, she made her way to the curious old house.

Marjorie found Mrs. Hotchkiss far more ill than when she had left her that afternoon, but she raised herself in bed when Marjorie went in, and taking her hand, she held it between both her own.

"That's right, dear!" she whispered. "I've been just longing for you to come. Send them out, and I'll tell you."

"I think she has something she wants to say to me," said Marjorie to Enoch and Peggie Jones, who were standing by the window; "if you would like to rest for a little, I will take care of her."

"Don't you mind being left, Miss?" said Peggy.

"Oh no, not at all; and I will call you if she is worse."

"Rap on that wall," said Peggy; "my bed is just on the other side of it, and I'll be with you in a moment. Our house joins this, you know."

They left the room together and went down the steep stairs, and presently Marjorie heard them closing the outer door, and she knew that she was alone in the house with the dying woman.

"Are they gone, my dear?" she asked.

"Yes, they are gone," said Marjorie.

"Are we quite alone?"

"Yes, quite alone."

"You know what you said about confessing?"

"Yes! 'If we confess our sins, He is faithful and just to forgive us our sins.'"

"I want to ask you something, dearie. Stoop your head down to me; I want to whisper. If you was to make a promise to somebody, and if it was a wicked promise that you had no business to have made, ought you to keep it?"

"Certainly not," said Marjorie. "It would be wrong to make a wicked promise, and it would also be wrong to keep it when you had made it."

"Do you think so, my dear? Are you sure?"

"Quite sure."

"Then listen, dearie, and I'll tell you. I feel as if I can't die till I do. I feel as if I must tell somebody. See? You know who Carrie is?"

"Yes; your daughter."

"Ay, and I wasn't half proud of her; a clever girl too, and such a scholar! Well, Carrie married a man as she met up in the North somewhere; and he was well-to-do and all that. I believe they had a very comfortable home, but he was awful mean to Carrie. He never would let her send anything to her poor old mother. I was nigh starved, my dear, I was indeed. If I hadn't raked in the ash-heaps, there's many a day I wouldn't have had a fire. I only had parish pay, see? And not too much of that. But one day they came to see me."

"Who did?"

"Her and her husband. And he spoke very fair, and he said if I would do a little thing for him, he'd allow me ten shillings a week as long as I lived. Well, my dear, I said I would do it, if I could. He wouldn't tell me what it was till I had promised I wouldn't tell anybody. And then he went to his hand-bag, and he brought out a tin box. It was just a common sort of box, like a small biscuit-box, and it had a bit of string tied tight round it.

"'Now, mother,' he says, 'I want you to hide this 'ere box in one of them little cupboards in the chimney corner till I send for it. I'm a-going to Ameriky,' he says, 'and when we're settled there and have got a home of our own, I'll write you word where to send it.'

"'Can't you take it with you?' I says. 'It isn't big, and it won't take much room in your boxes.'

"'No,' he says; 'I'd rather you sent it, mother, and I'll let you have the address. Old Enoch will direct it for you. You can tell him it's something as Carrie left behind her.'

"Well, my dear, it seemed a stroke of good luck for me, didn't it now? And then he said they must go; but Carrie begged and prayed him to let her stay just one night with me, as she was going so far away, and might never see her old mother again."

"And did he let her?"

"He wouldn't at first; but Carrie cried, my dear. And at last he gave in, and said she was to follow him the next day. Well, we went to bed, Carrie and me, dearie, and when she was lying beside me that night, I told her I did not much like having charge of that tin box, because folks might rob an old woman like me. And I asked her did she think it was jewels, or what was it?"

"What did she say?"

"She said it was naught but paper—some letters, she said—and then she began to cry. So I asked her what was the matter, dear. And she said she didn't like it at all; but they wouldn't listen to what she said."

"Who wouldn't?"

"Him and his sister. They'd stole this 'ere letter from some one as his sister lived with. She stole it, I believe, and then he took it and raised money on it."

"How could he do that?"

"I don't know, my dear. I can't understand these things. She called it 'hush money,' or some such name. There was somebody as didn't want what was in that letter to be known. And Josiah—that's my daughter's husband, dearie—kept on threatening him that he would tell, and then making him pay money to get him to hold his tongue. Carrie said that some day Josiah would sell this man the letter, and get hundreds of pounds for it; but he wanted first to see how much he could get out of him by threatening him, without parting with the letter."

"I wonder what it was about," said Marjorie.

"I don't know, my dear. Carrie didn't know; he wouldn't let her read it. And I've never opened the box, and I couldn't read it if I did."

"Then your daughter did not like what her husband was doing?"

"No; she was frightened, my dear. Mr. Forty Screws was in a great way about losing the letter. See? And Josiah was afraid he would put the 'tectives on them, so that's why they was going out of the country. His sister was going with them, his half-sister she was; she was the one that stole it from Mr. Forty Screws, and they didn't want to take the letter with them, lest the 'tectives should search them, and find it in their boxes. When once they got over to Ameriky they thought they was safe. See? Carrie did cry about it, though, my dear, and she said if she had her way she would give it back to Mr. Forty Screws, and have done with it all."

"What a curious name! Are you sure that it was Forty Screws?"

"Well, something like it, my dear."

"Where is the box?"

"In the cupboard below; one of those little cupboards by the fire."

"Then they never sent for it?"

"Never, dearie, and I haven't heard a word from them since; it's more than six months now since they sailed. There was a ship went down in them parts soon after they went; at least Enoch told me so. He saw it in the papers; and sometimes I think they all went down in it. I'm sure Carrie would have written if she'd been alive. Now I've told you, my dear. Have I done right, do you think?"

"Quite right, Mother Hotchkiss, and I think you ought to do more; you ought to send that letter back to the man from whom it was stolen."

"I don't know where he lives nor nothing about him, my dear; and then it seems mean, after taking Josiah's money, to go and tell of him."

"How can Josiah be drowned if he still sends you the money?"

"He doesn't send it now, my dear. He left enough to last for a year with Tom Noakes at the public there, and he pays it to me reg'lar, Tom does. Then Josiah said that he would send more when the year was up. See?"

"That letter ought certainly to go back to the man to whom it belongs," said Marjorie, "I am sure of that."

"But how can I tell who it is?"

"May I look at the letter? Perhaps his address is on it."

"Yes, my dear, you may if you like. Will you go and get it?"

Marjorie took the candle and went down the rickety stairs. A cold wind blew up from the vault-like dairy as she passed the flight of stone steps leading down to it. She felt almost like a thief herself, as she crossed the kitchen and made her way to the ancient fireplace. There was the old oak cupboard, the door of which had often attracted her attention by its quaint appearance.

The small cupboard was locked, but the key was in it. She turned it in the lock, and the carved door flew open. She hunted amongst the rubbish with which it was filled, but she found no box. Odds and ends of all descriptions were there, but nowhere could she discover the one thing she had come to seek.

Perhaps the letter was in the other cupboard. There was no key in that; but she found that she could open it with the key she had found in the first one. She unlocked it; and at first she thought that this second cupboard was empty; she could see nothing whatever in it.

However, as she felt along the shelf, she discovered in one corner of it, tightly jammed into the wall, and well out of sight, a small tin box. It took her some minutes to get it out, and then, by the light of her candle, she looked at it. It was tied up tightly with string, and the string was sealed in several places. She carried it upstairs and put it in the old woman's hands.

"Is that it?" she said.

"Yes, my dear, that's it. Will you open it?"

"I hardly like to do it," said Marjorie, "and yet—Did you say the name was Forty Screws? Do you think it possible, Mother Hotchkiss, that it could have been Fortescue?"

"Very likely, my dear; I never can remember names, only I thought of the screws in a box my old man used to keep 'em in. They're there yet, dear. And then I thought of forty of them. See? And I remembered it that way. But maybe I didn't hear her quite right, my dear."

Again Marjorie hesitated. But if it should be—if it was possible that it could be something that he had lost and that he wanted—something that he would be glad to have once more in his hands. Yes, she would open it; it could not be wrong—it surely could not be wrong.

She broke the seals and unfastened the string. Then it was easy to take off the lid of the box. Inside was a sheet of foolscap paper, closely covered with writing.

She glanced at the beginning, "My dear Ken."

She looked at the end, "Your loving Father, Joseph Fortescue."

Yes, it was the same! Even the handwriting was familiar to her; she had often seen it before when old Mr. Fortescue had written with the cheques which he sent to her mother.

Hastily she put the letter back in the box, closed the lid, and tied the string tightly round it; not a word of it should be seen by any one. She was trembling with agitation as she did so, and the old woman noticed it.

"You know him, my dear?"

"Yes, I know him," she said; but her teeth chattered as she spoke.

"You're cold, my dear."

"No, not cold, only so glad."

"Has he wanted it, my dear?"

"I expect so; he hasn't told me, but it may be everything to him just now, if it's good news. I hope it is."

"Will you take it to him, dear?"

"Shall I?"

"Yes, do, dear; don't tell anybody else, will you?"

"No, I won't; no one else shall know."

"Promise you'll take it to him yourself!"

"I promise."

"Now, my dear, I can say my prayer. I think He'll forgive me now."

"Yes," said Marjorie, as her tears fell fast, "dear Mother Hotchkiss, I know He will. 'If we confess our sins, He is faithful and just to forgive us our sins.' He is faithful, because He has promised to forgive us, and so you see, He can't say no when we ask Him; and He is just, because the Lord Jesus has been punished instead of us, and so God cannot punish us too for the same sins. Do you see?"

"Yes, my dear, thank you; I shall die happy now."

Soon after this, steps were heard on the stairs, and the old woman signalled to her to hide the box, and Marjorie slipped it under her coat just as Peggy Jones came into the room.

"You'll let me come now, Miss," she said. "You must be so tired. You ought to go home and get a bit of sleep."

Marjorie stooped down and kissed the poor old face lying on the pillow, and then she crept downstairs and went out into the darkness. But she did not mind even that to-night; she felt as if she cared for nothing, so long as the box was safe. When she got to the house the door had been left on the latch, so she let herself in and crept up to bed, carrying the precious box with her.

CHAPTER XV
156, LIME STREET

MARJORIE was wakened the next morning by hearing some one moving about in her room. She looked up and saw Patty standing near her bed, with a little tray in her hand.

"Miss Douglas, I've brought you your breakfast," she said. "Shall I draw up the blind?"

"Oh dear," said Marjorie, jumping up, "I had no idea it was so late; why did nobody wake me?"

"Mother wouldn't let us; she told us you had been up half the night."

"Yes, poor old Mrs. Hotchkiss sent for me."

"Miss Douglas, old Enoch has just been here, and he said we were to tell you she is dead. She went to sleep soon after you left her, and when Peggy Jones looked at her about an hour afterwards, she found that she was dead."

"Only just in time," said Marjorie to herself when Patty had gone, as she felt for the box which she had put under the bolster the night before. Yes, it was safe.

How she wondered what it contained! He must have it at once, without even a single day's delay; she would never be happy until it was safely in his hands. What if the old woman's son-in-law should return, and demand that what he considered to be his property should be given up to him? Perhaps, after all, he had never gone to America; perhaps he had deceived the old woman, in order that she might put the police off the scent, in case they came in search of him.

Marjorie was tired and depressed after her wakeful night, and fears of all kinds crowded into her mind. In her nervous haste she longed to run to the station at once, that she might catch the first train to Birmingham, and, carrying the precious box with her, find the address Kenneth had given her on his card, and at once rid herself of the heavy responsibility which she felt rested upon her, so long as that letter was in her charge.

But Marjorie could not go off thus hurriedly, without giving a sufficient reason to Mrs. Holtby, and she knew that the busy morning's work was already waiting for her.

She dressed quickly, therefore, and hurried downstairs. Never did she work so hard as on that morning; never did she try so earnestly to get ahead of time, or to cram the work of two hours into one. When dinner-time came, she had not only done the work of the morning, but she had finished the darning and the mending which she usually did on Friday afternoon, and had put by all the clean clothes from the weekly wash.

Mrs. Holtby came down just before dinner, and then Marjorie, with a beating heart, went to make her request. Would it be possible for her to be spared for half a day? There was a friend in Birmingham whom she particularly wished to see.

"But won't you be too tired to go to-day, Miss Douglas? You look very white, after your bad night."

"Oh no, I am not at all tired. I should like to go very much, if you can spare me. I have got on well this morning, and have done all the mending."

"You never neglect anything, dear."

It was the first time she had called her "dear," and the word had a home-like sound that went warm to Marjorie's heart.

Then Mrs. Holtby brought out the time-table, and looked out her train. There was one that left Deepfields at 2.30, and she told her to get her dinner at once, and not to wait till the others came in, so that she might be off in time to catch it.

"Don't hurry back, Miss Douglas," she said, when Marjorie looked in to say good-bye. "Stay as long as ever you like."

So, with the box wrapped in paper and tightly held in her hand, and with the card in which Captain Fortescue had given her slipped inside her glove, Marjorie set off for Deepfields.

It was a pouring wet day, and the mud was, if possible, worse than usual, but she hardly noticed it. She would have gone through a perfect flood without minding it, in her intense eagerness to get to her journey's end. How glad he would be to get that letter! How thankful he would feel that it was found at last!

But would he be glad and thankful? As she sat in the train a horrible fear crossed her mind. What if she were bringing him bad tidings? What if she were indeed what he had called himself—a bird of ill omen? She hoped not, she prayed not; but how could she tell?

Arrived at Birmingham, she found herself in all the bewilderment of New Street station at one of its most crowded moments. She took out the card, and looked at it once more—"156, Lime Street," that was the address. How should she find it? She asked a porter, who was wheeling a barrow of luggage, but he said he had never heard of it.

Then she went up the steps to the bridge, and felt in a perfect whirl as the busy crowds rushed past her. Hundreds of strange faces—all of them intent on their own business, and none of them having a moment to spare for hers: all these she saw as if she were in a dream. Which way should she turn at the top of the bridge? There seemed to be two exits to the station. Which should she take? She went to the one to which most people seemed to be going. It took her out into Corporation Street. All looked strange to her. She had no eyes for the beautiful shops; the Arcade failed to tempt her as she passed it. All she wanted was to get to her journey's end.

At last she met a policeman, and found from him that she was walking in the wrong direction. He sent her back almost to the station, and told her to take a turning to the left, and to walk on until she saw a large church, and then she must ask for further direction.

The rain was now coming down in torrents, and a strong wind was blowing in her face, but she struggled on bravely against it. She found the church at last, and went into a small shop to ask her way. Again she set forth, and walked on for another mile, and, after getting wrong once or twice, and stopping to inquire many times of the passers-by, she at last reached the street that she was seeking.

Lime Street was long and dismal-looking, with two rows of houses facing each other, all exactly alike, and all standing close to the pavement, with not even a pretence to a front garden. The street looked, if possible, more gloomy than usual that afternoon; in the merciless rain everything was wet, dirty, and uninviting.

Now for No. 156. It was at the other end of that long street, and she hurried on to find it. But as she got near, the thought of seeing him again, the doubt as to the news which she was bringing him, the strange feeling of responsibility which rested upon her in thus doing the bidding of one who had so lately passed away from earth—all these made her tremble and pause as she stood on the doorstep.

When she had steadied herself for a few moments she rang the bell, and a stout elderly woman came to the door.

"Is Captain Fortescue at home?" she asked. "Mr. Fortescue lodges here; he isn't a captain, Miss—but he's out just now."

"When will he be home?"

"Oh, not for long enough yet; he mostly comes in about six or half-past."

Marjorie looked at her watch; it was a quarter to four. Her heart died within her. Two hours and a quarter, or perhaps longer still. Where should she go, and what should she do till six o'clock? Where in those wet and dirty streets could she find a shelter?

The landlady was closing the door, but as she did so, she noticed the look of dismay on Marjorie's face.

"Have you come far, Miss?" she asked.

"Yes, a long way," said Marjorie, "from near Bilston, and I know nobody in Birmingham."

"Is it very particular?"

"Very; I must see Mr. Fortescue to-night."

"Come your ways in, then," said the woman, kindly; "there's a bit of fire in his sitting-room, if you would like to wait there."

Marjorie thanked her gratefully, and she led the way into a small room at the back of the house, and, after putting some coal on the fire, she told her to sit by it and warm herself after her cold, wet walk. Then, as she was going out, she noticed how drenched Marjorie's coat was, and made her take it off that she might dry it at her kitchen fire.

When the landlady was gone, Marjorie looked round the room. It was very plainly and even shabbily furnished. A worn horse-hair sofa stood against the wall, the deal table was covered with American cloth, the carpet was patched in several places.

Marjorie walked to the window and looked out. No wonder the room was dark! High buildings backed upon the house and shut out nearly all the light. Only a strip of cloudy sky could be seen above, whilst below was a small courtyard filled with clothes, which had evidently been put out to dry before the rain commenced, but which were now more soaked than they had been before, and hung dismally from the line stretched across from wall to wall of the small backyard.

How dull it all was! How poor, how depressing! She remembered his words to her mother, "I will not allow myself in a single indulgence of any kind, till the full amount is in your hands."

How faithfully he was keeping that promise! How bare of all luxury was the room to which he came home after his long tiring day!

But what was that over the chimney-piece,—a photo in a frame? It carried her miles away in thought as she looked at it, and a great feeling of home-sickness came over her.

It was a picture of Honister Crag.

CHAPTER XVI
THE BLOTTED WORD

HOW long the waiting-time seemed to Marjorie as she sat in the dingy back parlour on that wet afternoon! she felt sometimes as if six o'clock would never come. As it grew darker, the stout landlady came in and lighted the gas; there was only one burner, and it gave but a dim light. Then, later still, she came again to lay the cloth for tea. Such a poor scanty meal, the loaf and a small pat of butter—that was all. There were no flowers on the table, there was nothing to relieve the bareness and austere simplicity of it all. Marjorie's heart ached for him as she looked at it. What an utter contrast to the luxury in which she knew that he had lived before!

Mrs. Hall, the landlady, lingered when she had laid the table, and seemed inclined to talk.

"You'll excuse me, Miss," she said, "but are you Mr. Fortescue's sister?"

"No, not his sister."

"Well," she said, "I'm sorry you're not, because if he has a sister, I should like to have a bit of a talk with her. Somebody ought to come and look after him."

"Is he ill?" asked Marjorie, quickly.

"Well, no, not what you can call ill; but he soon will be, if he goes on as he's going on now."

"What do you mean?"

"Why, he doesn't get enough to eat; at least he has plenty to eat of a kind, but it isn't what a man like him, as is working hard all day, ought to have. Look at his tea now! It don't look as it ought, do it now? And his dinner! He has it out some days, and what he gets then I can't say; not much, I'll be bound; but some days, he comes home for it, and I assure you I'm fair shamed to get him the dinners he orders. One day it will be, 'Mrs. Hall, I'm very fond of herrings; do you think you could get me a couple of nice ones for my dinner?' Another day he'll say, 'Mrs. Hall, you make awfully good soup, I should like that better than anything to-day.'

"'And what to follow, sir?' I says. 'Oh, one of your nice rice puddings; that will be just the kind of dinner I like.' Another day it's sausage, or a bit of bacon, or bread and cheese, and not too much of any of them either. Why, my last lodger would clear off in one meal double what he eats in a day! And such a nice gentleman, too—always so pleasant, and thanks you for all you do for him just as if you didn't get paid for doing it. And so hard as he works, too! Why, if you'll believe me, he's at them books and accounts, and them business letters of his, long after I've gone to bed. I hear him come upstairs, and I know he's tired by his step, and well he may be, for he's tramping about most of his time."

Mrs. Hall loved a chat, and would have gone on for much longer enlarging on the many good qualities of her lodger, if she had not at that moment heard the sound of a key being put into the latch of the door.

"Why, there he is at last!" she said. "I'll go and make the tea."

Marjorie's heart was beating very quickly now. She heard the door open and Mrs. Hall's voice outside.

"Why, you're not half wet, sir. Let me take your coat."

Then the well-known voice: "Thank you, Mrs. Hall, it will be all the better for a dry by your fire."

"There's a lady waiting to see you, sir, in the parlour there; she's been here the best part of the afternoon."

"A lady for me!"

He stopped to ask no question, but came quickly into the room.

"Miss Douglas, you here!"

He had been thinking of her as he came up the street; he had been wondering how she was getting on in her hard life at Daisy Bank; and now here she was, in the very last place in which he would ever have dreamt of seeing her, sitting in the old armchair by the fire in his dismal little room. She rose to meet him, and at once held out the precious parcel.

"Captain Fortescue, I have come to bring you that. It is something which I think—I hope—you will be very glad to get."

He took the box in his hand but did not open it.

"What is it?" he asked. "Do sit down, Miss Douglas."

He noticed how agitated she was, and he wondered what had caused her to be so.

"Have you not lost something?" she asked.

"Only an umbrella," he said, laughing. "I lost one last week; but that can't be in here."

"No," she said, "it was much longer ago. Think, Captain Fortescue; did you never lose a letter that you wanted very much to find? Was a letter never stolen from you by some one? And have you not tried in all ways to find that letter, but in vain?"

He understood now: all the colour had faded from his face. Was it possible, could it be that his father's letter had been found—and by her?

"Is it in this box?" he asked.

"Yes; I do hope it is the right one. Will you open it and see?"

He cut the string which she had knotted tightly round it: he drew out the paper; he saw his father's well-known irregular handwriting.

Yes, it was evidently the letter which he ought to have found in that envelope in the safe, the envelope of which was still in his possession, and which was addressed, "For my son, To be opened after my death."

"Is it the right one?"

"Yes, it is, Miss Douglas. How can I thank you?"

"May I tell you how I found it? And then I must go."

She knew how he was longing to read the letter, and she thought that he would want to read it alone. Her one desire was to tell him how it had come into her possession, and then to leave him. But he would not hear of her doing this; he made her sit down again, and, before she could stop him, he rang the bell for Mrs. Hall, and told her to bring another cup, that she might have some tea before she left.

Then Marjorie told him her story as shortly as she could. She spoke of old Mrs. Hotchkiss's unhappiness during her illness; she told him of her midnight call to the old house, and of the secret that had then been told her. She described the place in which she had discovered the box; she confessed that she had broken the seals and opened it, that she might see the name at the end of the letter, and might know whether Mr. Forty Screws and Mr. Fortescue were the same. And now she said, as she got up from her chair again, she was thankful, very glad and thankful that it was safely in his hands, and she must go; she really must go. She knew how he was longing to read it, and she would not keep him another moment.

"Miss Douglas," said Captain Fortescue, "I am not going to allow you to leave until you've had some tea, and then I am going with you to the station. But if you are sure you do not mind, I will just read the letter, and then I shall be able to tell you what it is about, and for what I have to thank you."

When she saw that it was of no use to protest any further, she sat down again by the fire, and he took a chair to the table, and by the dim light of the solitary gas-burner sat down to read the letter. She glanced at him from time to time as he bent over it, wondering as she did so what its contents might be, looking anxiously to see the effect upon him as he read. Every vestige of colour had faded out of his face, but he read on intently, and without once looking up. Marjorie could hear the clock in the passage ticking loudly, but no other sound disturbed the stillness of the room. He did not speak a word, nor utter a sound, till he turned to the last page, and then he gave a loud exclamation of dismay.

"Is it bad news?" she asked fearfully.

"No, not bad news; it is good news, very good news," he said, "but those rascals have tampered with the letter."

He held it up to her, and she saw that one word, a long word too, had been completely blotted out.

"It has evidently been done on purpose," he said, "lest this letter should by any means fall into my hands."

"Is the word of much importance?"

"Of every importance; in fact, it is the most important word in the whole letter. Miss Douglas, we will have some tea, and then I want you, if you do not mind, to read the letter you have brought."

"May I? But are you sure you would like me to read it?"

"I am quite sure; indeed, so far from minding it, I am most anxious that you should read it."

He put the armchair near the table for her, and began to pour out the tea, but his hand trembled so much with strong emotion that she asked him if she might do it for him. He told her that, if she did not mind doing it, he should like to remember it, after she had gone; it would be something to think of when he was alone.

"It's rather different to the last tea we had together," he said; "that cosy tea in Fernbank. If I had known you were coming, I would have had some cake!"

But at that moment Mrs. Hall came into the room with a hot tea-cake in her hand.

"I've just baked 'em, sir, and they're nice and light, and I thought, as the lady was here, perhaps you would accept of one."

"Thank you, Mrs. Hall; it looks delicious!" They did not talk much during tea; his mind was on the letter he had just read, and he asked her from time to time to give him further details of the history which she had heard from Mrs. Hotchkiss. He had no doubt whatever that Makepeace was the man who had married Carrie Hotchkiss, and he remembered hearing that Watson had a half-brother living in Sheffield. Evidently, then, he had been right in his former suspicion; Watson had undoubtedly been the thief. She must have been listening at the bedroom door when his father told him to look under the will in the safe for the important letter which he wished him to receive.

Then, when she found herself alone with the old man for the night, she must have taken the keys from the table whilst he was asleep, unlocked the safe, and taken out the letter, replacing it, either then or afterwards, by a blank sheet of foolscap paper. Then, when she had satisfied her curiosity, and had also discovered the importance of its contents, she had evidently carried the letter to Makepeace, and the brother and sister must have plotted together that they would keep it back, in the hope that they might be able to make it a kind of gold mine, were they fortunate enough to discover the father who had deserted his infant child.

They could not help being aware that the information in the letter was of such a nature that it would be of the utmost importance to that man to have it suppressed.

Then, after that, Watson must have found that other letter, the one Makepeace had brought him, lying unposted on the table, and then either she or her brother must have invented the plausible story which Makepeace had told him, in order to prevent any suspicion from falling upon Watson.

All this probable explanation of the strange mystery flashed through Kenneth Fortescue's mind more quickly than it can be told here, and Marjorie could see that from time to time his thoughts were far away, although he always seemed to notice in a moment if she wanted anything, and he was not content until she had done justice to Mrs. Hall's tea-cake. He ate very little himself, and, as soon as she had finished, he drew her chair nearer to the fire and handed her the letter.

"Are you quite sure you want me to read it?" she asked again. "Do say if you would rather I did not."

"It will be a comfort to me if you do not mind reading it, Miss Douglas."

She could not refuse after that. She unfolded the large sheet and began to read.

CHAPTER XVII
A STRANGE LETTER

THE letter which Marjorie held in her hand was badly written and spelt, but she was able to decipher most of it. And this is what she read—

"MY DEAR KEN,

"I feel as if I might not live for many years longer, so I am writing this, that you may be able to read it when I am dead and gone. I feel as if I ought to let you know; and yet I promised him to keep his secret as long as I lived, all the days of my life, them was the words as he made me say. But I didn't promise not to tell when the days of my life was over, Ken, and they will be over when you get this 'ere letter.

"Well, Ken, I'm a-going to tell you something that happened to me about twenty-five years ago. I heard as there was good luck to be had out in South Africa; so me and your ma talked it over, and we settled we would go out there and make our fortunes. We had saved a bit of money, and we paid our passage, and we went out, and we got on pretty fair. The work was good, and so was the pay, but things was a lot dearer out there than at home.

"I worked on, Ken, first in one place and then in another, and at last we settled down near some mines not far from Kimberley. There were a lot of miners there, a rough set most of them, and the life was a pretty hard one. I made good money there, though I spent it pretty nigh as fast as I made it. We got a decent sort of a house, and your ma took a pride in it, and I bought some furniture of a man who was going to England, and we fed on the fat of the land. It was when we was there that I got a man, who had been a painter afore he left England, to paint a big picture of my missus, and I paid him well for doing it. That's it as hangs in the library, Ken. Well, it was while we was living there in a ramshackle sort of town, that one night, after dark, Jack McDougall, him as kept the Inn there, came to our house.

"'Joe,' he says, 'here's a nice job we're in for at our house. Here's a gent, as is travelling on to Kimberley, and he came to our house with a lady last night, and now there's the lady ill in bed, and a little baby born in the night. And doctor, him from over yonder, has just been here, and he says she's very bad and going to die.'

"'That's a bad job, Jack!' I says.

"'Yes, Joe,' he says, 'and my missus is that scared she don't know what to do, and there's nobody else about but old Nurse Grindle, and she's half drunk. So I came across to see if your missus would come over and help us a bit.'

"Well, your ma went; she were that handy when folks were ill, and she did what she could for the poor lady; but it weren't of no use, and the next day she died. My missus was fair cut up when she had passed away; she said she had the prettiest face and the loveliest hair she had ever seen, and she looked so young too! Your ma brought the baby over to our house, such a poor little thing it was! Doctor said he didn't think it had a chance to live. Well, we said we would keep it till after the funeral, but that night, when I was just a-going to bed, I heard some one at the door.

"I went down, and there was a fine-looking gentleman, the handsomest man I've ever seen excepting one, and that's yourself, Ken! I guessed it was the baby's father, and I asked him if he would come in. I thought he had come to fetch his child, and I told him my missus had taken it up to bed, but I would tell her he had come for it. He said, 'No, he hadn't come for the baby; but he had come to talk to me.' So I asked him in, and we sat over the fire together.

"He did not speak at first, and then he said, 'How would I like to be a very rich man?' I said as how I would like it very much, nothing better. And then he said he could put me in the way of being one if I liked; he could make a gentleman of me, and I would never have to work any more. You can think I opened my ears then, Ken, and I asked him how he was going to manage it, and what he wanted me to do. He didn't answer for a bit, and then he said he would tell me. He wanted me and my missus to take charge of the baby.

"'For how long?' I asked.

"'For always,' he said. 'I want it to stop with you altogether, if so be that it lives, which it won't do; the doctor gives it three months at most. Still, there's just the chance it may! So I want you to adopt it, in fact,' he says.

"I thought it was awfully queer of him, Ken, to want to get rid of his own child; it seemed to me unnatural-like, so I asked him why he did it. He told me he was in a bit of a difficulty, and this would help him out of it. I said I wouldn't do it unless he told me what the bother was. So then he went so far as to say his father had written him a letter, and that letter obliged him to do it. But I wasn't satisfied, Ken; I said I must know what the letter was about, and then it all came out.

"'His father, he said, was a very wealthy man in England, who had married an American lady with a big fortune of her own. His father had a grand estate somewhere, and of course he was the heir to it; his mother was dead, and all her money, having been settled on herself, had come to him; but of course it was nothing to what he would get when his father died. However, his father had married again about a year ago, and this second wife had a child, also a boy.

"Then he went on to tell me that his father had for a long time set his heart on his marrying a lady who owned the next estate. She had one of the biggest rent-rolls in England, and if he married her, they would own the whole county between them. She was older than he was, but he had no objection to marrying her now, in fact, he thought it was the best thing he could do; but of course she would never dream of having him, if she had any idea that he had been married before, or had a child living who would be heir to his title and estates. I asked him why he had objected to marrying this lady before, and he said it was because he liked some one else better,—this wife of his who had just died.

"He had been married abroad, and his father knew nothing about her. She was the daughter of a Chaplain at one of the places he had stopped at. I told him if he was so fond of his wife, he ought to be fond of her child; but he said the child had cost her her life, and how could he bear to look at it? He felt as if he never wanted to see it again. Besides, it was no use talking about the child. If he was to take it back to England (and how could he possibly travel with so young a baby?) what would his father say? He had had a letter from his father, in which he told him that, if he didn't do as he wanted him about marrying this girl (or this woman, whatever she was) that lived near them, he would leave all his money to the little boy—the child of his second wife. He couldn't leave him the title or the estate; they had to go to the eldest son; but he could leave his money to whoever he liked.

"Well, Ken, he talked and he argued half the night, and at last I called my missus, and told her to get up and come downstairs. She didn't like the thought of it at first; it seemed like cheating the poor child, she said, and keeping him out of his rights. But he offered us a big sum of money, a fortune, Ken, half of what he'd got from his mother, that rich American lady, if I would only say I would keep the child, and at last me and my missus came round. She told him he was a heartless man, and she didn't like doing it; but you see the money was a big temptation, Ken. Never to have to work any more and to live like grand folks, seemed almost more than we could put aside. And then we had no children of our own, and the missus had always wanted one, and she were kind of wrapped up in this little baby.

"Well, the end of the matter was, that we said we would consent, and then he made me take a solemn promise that I wouldn't ever tell anybody that it wasn't my own child, but that I would keep his secret all the days of my life.

"He asked me then what my name was, and I said Tomkins, and he laughed and said, 'Give the poor little beggar a better-sounding name than that. Change your name, Tomkins,' he says, 'to something that sounds a bit more aristocratic than that.'

"'What shall it be, sir?' I says. 'I'm not going to tell you, Tomkins, nor do I want to know,' he says. 'Get a pen and I'll write you out a cheque; but no, that won't do!' he says. Then he sits and thinks a bit. You see, Ken, he didn't want me to know his name nor who he was, and the cheque would have told me. 'I know,' he says at last, 'I'll cash the cheque myself, and bring you the money; they can easily wire to my English bankers from the Kimberley Bank, and they'll find it's all right.'

"So a day or two after that he brings the money, Ken,—a great roll of notes it was, and each note was for £100. He counted it all out, what he'd agreed to give me; and then he said he was going to give me £5000 extra, for the poor little beggar, in case he lived. He would like him to be educated as a gentleman, he said. I think his conscience had smote him, Ken.

"Well, I promised that I would do the best I could for the baby, and then my missus said should she fetch it, that he might give it a kiss, but he said No, he thought he had rather not see it. He was a heartless man,—very.

"Then I asked him, Ken, if I might know his name and address, in case I had anything to tell him about the baby. How could I let him know if it died or anything happened to it? But he said there was no need to let him know, and he did not intend to tell me his name. I had got my money, and what more did I want?

"Well, he got up to go, and I helped him to put on his coat, for it was raining when he came, and then I noticed for the first time that he had something the matter with his hand; the last joint of the little finger of the right hand was gone. After that he went away, and I've never seen him, Ken, from that day to this. I went to the Inn, and I found that there he had given the name of Vavasour, but I feel sure that was not his right name; he was far too clever for that.

"However, some time after, I came across a man who had travelled out with him from England—at least I think it must have been the same, from this man's description of him and his wife. He told me that these people he had met were going out to South Africa, and he wondered whether they had ever come to Kimberley. He told me that the man was a lord, and that some one on board ship, who had seen him before, said that he was the son of—"

Here came the word or words which had been so carefully blotted out.

"Now, Ken, what I've got to tell you is this. That man was your father, and you are that poor little deserted boy. I've done my best for you, Ken; you know as I have. I had a hard time with you at first, for we started off for England when you was about two months old, and before we got halfway home, my poor missus died, your ma as you have always called her; and there was I on board ship, left with a tiny weakly baby.

"But I reared you, Ken, and you lived and grew strong, in spite of yon old doctor at Kimberley, and now you're a fine handsome young man, and I love you as if you was my own son. But I would like for you to have your rights, Ken. Find that man if you can, and tell him he's your father. If he has any conscience, (he hasn't much, I'm afraid), he'll be obliged to own you, when you show him this letter, and tell him how you got it. And mark this, Ken, you're as like your father as two peas are like. I mean to say you're like what your father was when I saw him. Now he will be a man over fifty, I should say.

"Follow this up, Ken, and don't rest till you're got your rights.

"Your loving father,

"JOSEPH FORTESCUE.

"P.S.—I chose Fortescue because I thought as it sounded like the name of a gentleman."

CHAPTER XVIII
WORDS TO BE REMEMBERED

MARJORIE did not speak whilst she was reading the whole of that long letter, and Kenneth Fortescue sat and watched her, just as before she had sat and watched him. He saw her face flush as she read on, and once he felt sure that he saw a tear drop on the page. When at last she handed him the letter, she said—

"How could he be so cruel? It was awfully heartless, wasn't it?"

"Yes, it was most unnatural; but such things have been done before. Even a mother has been known to desert her own child."

"I wonder if he is alive."

"So do I. If only that word had been there!"

"Let us look at it carefully," Marjorie said; "perhaps we can make it out."

They bent together over the paper, as they held it in the light of the lamp.

"It must be a very long name," she said. "Can it all be one word? I think Lord is the first part of it. That looks to me like part of the loop of the L left above the blot."

"Yes, I think you are right. Even so, I think it is a long name—ten or twelve letters, I should say."

"Oh, I wish we knew!" said Marjorie.

"I wish it very much for one reason, Miss Douglas."

"What is that?"

"If I were to find my father, and if he were prepared to own me, or were compelled to do so, I could repay Mrs. Douglas in full."

"Oh, why are you always thinking of that? You must not do so," she said. "You are stinting yourself and making your life miserable, just for us. And it isn't right. Oh, it isn't right!"

She was crying now; she could not help it. The thought of his constant self-denial, the remembrance of the hardships that he was bearing for their sakes, even though the debt had never been his; the recollection of all this touched her so deeply that she found it impossible to keep back her tears.

"This letter alters everything," she said; "do think of that. Even if you felt yourself bound to repay us when you thought you were Mr. Fortescue's son, you cannot feel so now. He was never your father except in name. Do remember that, and do give up, once for all, the idea of giving us that money back. The loss of it had nothing to do with you, nor with any one at all belonging to you."

"I cannot look at it in that light, Miss Douglas," he said. "If he was merely my father in name, still he was, at the same time, the only father I have ever known. God helping me, that debt shall be paid."

"Captain Fortescue."

"Yes, Miss Douglas."

"I'm afraid that letter is not of much use, after all."

"It may be," he said. "Who can tell?"

She sat looking into the fire for some minutes without speaking, and then she said—

"I rather hope—" and then stopped.

"You rather hope what, Miss Douglas?"

"Oh, never mind. I did not mean to say it aloud. It was only a foolish thought which had no business to come into my mind."

"What was it?"

"Oh!" she said, laughing through her tears. "Such a silly thing! I was going to say that I rather hoped you were not a lord."

"Why not?"

"Oh, I don't know. I only thought we should not feel that you were quite so much our friend. It was very foolish, I know. Only you would seem so different to us then."

"Should I? I hope not," he said, gravely.

"And now I really must be going. What time is it, Captain Fortescue?"

He looked at, his watch, and they found it was getting late, so he got her coat, and she said good-bye to the old landlady, and they set out for New Street. Then he went for her ticket, and put her into the train, and just before it started, he stepped into the carriage and sat down beside her.

"Won't the train be off soon?" she asked. "Yes. I am coming with you."

"Coming with me? Why?"

"I'm not going to allow you to walk alone along that dark road from Deepfields Station at this time of night," he said.

"Oh, I shall be quite all right; you really mustn't come. You will be so tired, and it is not at all necessary. Please don't come."

But he would take no refusal. There would be plenty of time for him to catch the last train, he said, and Marjorie felt sure that, when he had once made up his mind about anything, there would be no possibility of moving him from it.

They talked of the letter most of the way from the station, and as they went through Daisy Bank she pointed out the dark cottage where the still form of the old woman was lying on the bed upstairs.

"How strange to think that my letter has been near you all this time!" he said.

Then they got to Colwyn House, and at the gate, he said good-bye. But before he left her he took her hand between both his own, and said in a whisper, as he held it for a moment—

"Thank you for all you have done for me to-day."

The next instant he was gone, and Marjorie let herself in with her latchkey. She found that Mr. and Mrs. Holtby were having supper. They wanted her to join them, but she said she was tired, and would rather go to bed.

She fell asleep as soon as her head touched the pillow, and she dreamt that his hands were still holding her own, and she thought that she could still feel their pressure as he said those words, which would ever remain in her memory as long as life should last.

"Thank you for all you have done for me to-day."

CHAPTER XIX
GRANTLEY CASTLE

Two months after her visit to Birmingham, Marjorie was standing on the platform at Daisy Bank, waiting for the Wolverhampton train. How impatient she was to start!

How full of happiness was her face on that December morning! For she was going home for Christmas. She could hardly believe that it was only a year since she had seen the dear home faces, and to have a whole month with them all seemed almost too good to be true. Patty had come with her to the station, and was full of regret at her departure, full of promises to take her place in the holidays, and to do all she could to keep the house tidy and clean.

As Marjorie looked at her, she could not help feeling that the last few months had made Patty quite a different girl. The brusqueness of her manner was gone; she was more happy and more contented, and, in leaving her in charge of the children and her mother, Marjorie felt that she was leaving one who would tread, as far as possible, in her footsteps; and as Patty would not have to go to school during the time of her absence, she would be able to keep all things as Marjorie had left them, and to save her mother from having any extra work. Thus Marjorie was going home with a happy heart, prepared to thoroughly enjoy her well-earned holiday.

Perhaps our thoughts are never more busily occupied than when we are travelling. As our bodies are being rapidly carried over miles of distance, our thoughts wander further still. As our eyes gaze out of the carriage window upon the various scenes through which we are passing, the eyes of our mind are gazing at other scenes, it may be in far-distant lands. We see the views around us as if we saw them not, for the inner pictures are so vivid that they eclipse the outward ones. As we glance at our fellow-passengers, ensconced with newspaper or book in the corners of the carriage, we are looking, it may be, at other faces and hearing other voices, far away from us in bodily presence, but very near and constantly present to our inner sight.

Marjorie's thoughts were very busy that cold wintry day. Not only was she full of anticipation, picturing out to herself the joy of arriving at home and seeing again the friends from whom she had so long been parted; but at times, as she travelled on, her thoughts, instead of flying northwards far ahead of the train, travelled southwards, and found their way to a little back sitting-room in a dingy street in Birmingham.

What was Kenneth Fortescue doing that day? Was he still living in that poor dismal neighbourhood? Was he still denying himself in countless different ways for their sakes? Or had he discovered the missing word in the letter? Had he found the father who had cast him off as a child? Had he been owned and reinstated in his rightful position? Perhaps he had; perhaps now he was taking his place amongst the great ones of the earth, and they would hear of him no more.

But no; in that case he would write to her mother, she was sure of that. If he was rich and was able to do so, that money would be repaid. She knew that he would never forget his promise, and that the revelation made to him in that letter would in no way alter his former determination. What if her mother had already heard from him? What if she were keeping the secret as a pleasant surprise for her on her return? So her busy thoughts wandered on, as the busy engine, puffing hard at times as they got into the hilly country of the North, bore her onwards towards Cumberland.

Then, as she drew nearer home, her thoughts were all centred on Keswick station. Who would be there to meet her? Which of the home faces would she see first? How eagerly she gazed out of the window long before the station came in sight! How anxiously she scanned the platform as the train began to stop!

Yes, there they were, her mother and Phyllis and Louis Verner. It seemed too good to be true! What a drive home that was, and how much they had to say to each other! How beautiful it all looked! She had never thought that the mountains were so high, or the Lake so lovely, or Borrowdale so fine, or Castle Crag so magnificent. She had loved them all from her childhood; but she thought she had never fully appreciated them until that day.

And then they reached home, her dear cosy home, so free from smoke and dirt and everything ugly or depressing. Little Carl was at the gate. How he had grown since she saw him last! And Leila was at the door, looking much better and stronger, and old Dorcas came running out of the kitchen to welcome her. And now she was in the cheerful dining-room, how lovely it all was! The table seemed laden with good things. It was all so tasteful and pretty, and it was home, and that was best of all.

The days flew very quickly after that. There were so many friends to be seen, there was so much to be said and to be done, that the first ten days seemed to fly on the wings of the wind. Old Mary and her other old women were overjoyed to see her, and sometimes she felt as if she had never really been away. Daisy Bank appeared to her like a dream from which she had awakened.

She went alone one day up the steep pass towards Honister Crag, and thought of the photo which she had seen over the mantlepiece at Birmingham. She wondered where he had bought it, and why he had chosen it. Was it in remembrance of the walk they had had there together? Oh no, of course it could not have been that. It was a beautiful place, and any one who had seen it would be glad to have a picture of it.

Marjorie was charmed to find how well Phyllis had taken her place in her absence. She had shaken off to a great extent the natural indolence of her nature, and had risen to the occasion in a way which Marjorie would hardly have thought possible. Her mother had been cared for and Leila had been waited on, almost as well as Marjorie had done it before she left home, and she felt that she would go back to Daisy Bank with a happy heart, knowing that all was going on well in the home she had left.

Louis Verner was, of course, a constant visitor at Fernbank, and was just the same easy, good-natured fellow as he had ever been. He was now in his third year at Oxford, and was still trying to discover his vocation. His father, however, declared that if Louis came to no decision during that vacation, he should settle the matter for him. It was finally decided that Louis should try to get into the Consular Service, and should sit for an examination to be held the following year. Whether he would be able to succeed in this was, Marjorie thought, extremely doubtful, for Louis had no love for work, and went through life doing as little of it as he possibly could. His motto seemed to be that Irish one which advises you to 'Take it easy, and if you can't take it easy, take it as easy as you can;' and it needs one of life's hardest and sternest lessons, to make men like Louis Verner realize its importance, and shake themselves free from their natural inclination to slackness and inertion.

Nevertheless, Louis was a most amusing companion and a good-hearted affectionate fellow, too affectionate sometimes, Marjorie thought; but she made fun of all his pretty speeches, and treated him, as she always had done, with sisterly candour. He did not mind what she said to him, although she spoke very plainly to him at times, and they were ever the best of friends.

But when Marjorie had been at home about a fortnight, something happened which brought a great cloud over her happiness.

"A letter for you, Marjorie," said Phyllis, who had gone to meet the postman at the gate, "and it has such a black border."

Marjorie took it hastily from her; she knew the writing well; it was Patty Holtby's. Such terrible news the letter contained, poor Patty had been almost broken-hearted as she wrote it. Her father had gone to the works the day before, apparently quite well, but a short time after he arrived there, he had been seen to stagger and fall, and when they went to him, they found that he was dead. It had been an awful shock to them all, and Patty said that she could hardly yet believe that it was true.

Marjorie felt as if all the brightness of her holiday had passed away. She realized now how fond she had become of the people with whom she had lived for the last year, and she longed to be with them in their time of trouble. She wrote at once, offering to return immediately if it would be the least comfort to them; she would only be too glad to come to them.

Marjorie waited anxiously for the answer. It came in poor Mrs. Holtby's writing. It would be an unspeakable help to have her there, she said, but their plans were so undecided now that she thought it would be better for her to wait for a few days. Her brother had come for the funeral, and he was helping her to arrange matters, and she would write again shortly.

When Mrs. Holtby's next letter came, it was a very sad one. She was grieved to have to say that it would be impossible for Marjorie to return to them. They were leaving Daisy Bank, and her brother, who was now a widower, had invited them to come and live with him. Of course now she would have to be very careful of expense, and could no longer afford to have a mother's help. She added that she could never thank Miss Douglas enough for all she had done for them; she would miss her more than words could say; but she felt sure that she would rejoice to know that Patty had profited so much by the good training she had received from her, that she was becoming the greatest comfort and help to them all. She ended by saying that she could hardly bear to think that Marjorie was not coming back to them; it was one of the most painful consequences of her heavy bereavement.

So that chapter of Marjorie's life was ended. Daisy Bank was, as far as she was concerned, nothing but a memory of the past. Never more would she climb the pit mounds, or watch old Enoch tending his roses, or walk amongst the furnace débris. A year ago she would not have believed that she would have felt the parting so much as she did, nor that she would have so many pleasant remembrances of their Black Country.

Now she must begin life again somewhere, and where would it be? She dreaded the thought of going once more amongst strangers, and even Colwyn House had become a kind of second home to her. Well, she must not be faint-hearted; she had been guided so far, and she knew that her Guide would not forsake her.

But January passed away, and February came, and no opening had been found for her. Marjorie was beginning to feel anxious on the subject of the family finance, when one day, returning from a walk, she found Colonel Verner's carriage at the door.

Louis had long since returned to Oxford, and Mrs. Verner was an invalid and not able to call, so she was somewhat surprised to see the carriage, and wondered whom she should see when she went into the house.

She heard voices in their little drawing-room, and her mother came to the door and culled her in. Marjorie found Colonel Verner, and with him a lady whom she had never seen before. The Colonel introduced Marjorie, and she found that the lady's name was Mrs. St. Hellier, the Honourable Mrs. St. Hellier, she discovered afterwards. She was Colonel Verner's cousin, and she was spending a few weeks with him at Grange.

Mrs. St. Hellier seemed an exceedingly pleasant woman, and Marjorie felt much drawn to her. After a little conversation on general subjects, she told them that a friend of hers was most anxious to find some one who would be willing to act as companion to her daughter. This young lady had met with an accident in the hunting-field, and was confined to her room, or rather to her rooms, for she was wheeled on an invalid couch into an adjoining apartment where she lay during the day, unable to move or to raise herself from her recumbent position.

The poor girl of course felt the confinement; the monotony of such an existence was a sad change for her, after the active life which she had been accustomed to lead, and her mother was therefore anxious to find some one who would be willing to come to them as her daughter's companion. She would have no work of any kind to do; the lady's maid would undertake, as usual, all that was necessary in dressing and otherwise waiting upon her daughter. She simply wanted one who would be a cheerful companion, and who would be ready to read to her, to amuse her, and to turn her thoughts as much as possible from her helpless condition.

Then Mrs. St. Hellier went on to say that she had heard from Colonel Verner that Miss Douglas was looking for something of the kind, and she wanted to know whether she would like her to name her to Lady Earlswood. She thought she was at liberty to tell her that the remuneration would be a handsome one; fifty pounds a year was the amount mentioned by Lady Earlswood when she spoke to her on the subject.

Marjorie felt that this was indeed an answer to the prayers she had offered, and she gratefully accepted Mrs. St. Hellier's proposal that she should write to her friend without further delay.

In the course of the following week, Marjorie received a kind letter from Lady Earlswood, and in a very short time, all the preliminary arrangements were made, and she once more took leave of her home, and set off for Grantley Castle.

What a wonderful contrast she found on her arrival to her reception at Daisy Bank! A footman with a cockade on his hat came up to her on the platform, and told her that he would see after her luggage, and that the carriage was outside waiting for her. During the five miles' drive to the Castle, Marjorie leant back amongst the cushions of the luxuriously comfortable brougham, and wondered very much what was in store for her in the new home to which she was going.

When the carriage stopped, she was taken through the marble hall, and at the top of the long flight of steps, she found the housekeeper awaiting her.

"Lady Earlswood is out this afternoon, Miss Douglas," she said, "so she asked me to receive you. May I take you to your room? You will find a good fire, I think, and I will send you some tea in a few minutes. Lady Violet has had tea, so perhaps you would like to have it in your own room."

Marjorie thanked her, and followed her up the wide staircase into the bedroom which she was henceforth to call her own. It was not a large room, but it was most beautifully furnished. A pretty French bedstead, with dainty rosebud-covered hangings, a comfortable sofa covered with the same delicate chintz, an easy-chair by the bright fire, a writing-table, with inkstand, blotter and pens, at which she would be able to write her home letters—all these made Marjorie feel that she had come to a home where comfort and ease abounded.

Then she went to the window. It was not yet dark, and she could see hills and woods in every direction, whilst close to the house were three long terraces, one above another, from the various heights of which glorious views of the surrounding country could be obtained. What a strange contrast to the views from her bedroom window in Colwyn House!

Then there came a knock at the door, and a maid brought in a tray, on which was a small silver tea-pot and cream-jug, a china cup and saucer, and a plate of delicately cut bread and butter. It seemed strange to Marjorie to be thus waited upon, for she had been waiting upon others all her life, and as she sat in the armchair by the fire, pouring out the tea which had been placed on a small table beside her, she felt that, so far as she could see at present, the lines had indeed fallen for her in pleasant places.

CHAPTER XX
THE PHOTO OF A FRIEND

WHEN Marjorie first saw Lady Violet, she thought that hers was the most beautiful face that she had ever seen; yet she was very pale, and had a weary look in her eyes which told of pain and weakness. She held out her hand as Marjorie entered.

"Miss Douglas, I am glad to see you."

Marjorie took the low chair by Lady Violet's side, and told her that she hoped she would tell her exactly what she would like her to do, and that she would let her help her in any way that she could.

"Oh! I don't want you to do anything," she said, "only to amuse me. I'm so sick of seeing nobody but Collins; my mother and sister come up as often as they can, but we have so many visitors, and they have so many calls to make, and there is so much going on of one kind and another, that they are obliged to leave me hours alone sometimes. This is my worst time; I get so tired in the evening, and awfully cramped with lying so long in one position. You mustn't mind if I am cross sometimes; I often am."

Marjorie laughed, and told her she did not think that was possible.

"Oh, but it is. I worry poor Collins to death. Now I am tired and can't talk; will you talk to me?"

Marjorie found it very difficult to know what to say. It is one thing to join in a conversation, and quite another thing to talk to a silent person without having anything particular to say. She could not imagine how to begin, and then a bright thought struck her.

"Shall I tell you about my home, Lady Violet?"

"Yes, do; it will be just like a story."

So Marjorie began by describing Borrowdale and their pretty house on the hill; she told her about her mother, Leila, Phyllis, and little Carl; she spoke of the garden with its spring flowers, of the walk through the woods to Watendlath, at the top of the hill, of the quiet village church, of her old women and the quaint cottages in which they lived, of her life at home and of how she spent her days;—all this she told her, in her own bright, pleasant way, until the poor girl beside her was soothed and interested, and forgot her pain and weariness whilst she listened.

"Thank you," she said, when Marjorie stopped. "I can see it all as if I had been there. May I have another chapter to-morrow evening, and will you call Collins now to help me into bed? And do you mind telling me your Christian name?? I should like to call you by it if I may; Miss Douglas sounds so formal."

"Please do; my name is Marjorie. I shall feel I am at home, Lady Violet, if I hear you say it."

As the weeks went on, Marjorie soon became accustomed to her new life in the Castle. Beyond going for a walk daily in the lovely park and gardens, she spent all her time with Lady Violet. They had meals together in the pretty sitting-room, and Marjorie saw very little of the other members of the family. When they came to see Lady Violet, she generally went into her bedroom to write her letters, or strolled along one of the grassy terraces, or gathered primroses and moss in the copse wood to adorn Lady Violet's room.

By degrees, very slow degrees at first, Lady Violet let her companion know a little of what her thoughts and feelings were. She had been most reserved at first, and at one time Marjorie had felt as if she would never really know her. But one evening, when Marjorie had been at Grantley Castle about a month, the ice was broken for the first time. Lady Violet had been very restless and impatient all day; nothing was right that was done for her; she found fault with every one, and Marjorie herself experienced some difficulty in keeping bright and cheerful when all her efforts to cheer the patient seemed such an utter failure.

But after dinner, when Marjorie was sitting beside her with her work in her hand, Lady Violet suddenly said—

"Marjorie, I've been horrid all day; why don't you tell me so?"

Marjorie laughed. "Do you want a scolding?" she said.

"I don't mind one from you; but I do think it's a shame, a horrible shame."

"What is a shame?" asked Marjorie.

"My being laid on my back like this. Do you know, Marjorie, I was to have been married in May?"

"Oh, I'm so sorry," said Marjorie. "I had not heard about it."

"Oh, didn't you know? We were going to London to get my trousseau the very week that this accident happened. We were making all the plans about the wedding, and actually had patterns in the house for choosing the bridesmaids' dresses; and now here I am, lying helpless on my back, and my wedding put off indefinitely. It is an awful shame!"

"Don't say that, Lady Violet," said Marjorie, "because God has sent the trouble; hasn't He?"

"Then I think God is very cruel! What pleasure can it be to Him to punish me like this?"

"He doesn't like to see you suffer, Lady Violet. Oh, don't ever think that! It is because He loves you He has let this trouble come."

"I don't see much love in it! I suppose you mean that God thinks I need punishing; but I've never done anything to deserve it, and I do think it's a horrid shame!"

"Oh, don't say that!" said Marjorie. "Dear Lady Violet, don't say that!"

"But I must say it," she answered impatiently, "because I feel it, and it does me good to come out with it."

Marjorie did not speak for a few minutes, and Lady Violet said—

"Talk to me, Marjorie, scold me, if you like, only don't sit quiet like that. Tell me what you were thinking about."

"I was thinking about the eagle's nest, and that you were like one of the eaglets."

"What do you mean by that?"

"You know how the eagle makes her nest on the ledge of some high rock, building it of sticks and briars, and then lining it with moss, and hay, and wool, and soft feathers out of her own breast."

"Well," said Lady Violet, as Marjorie stopped, "go on."

"And then she lays her eggs, and the eaglets are hatched, and they lie down in the soft nest, and are so cosy that they never want to leave it. But, as they grow older, the mother-bird wants them to learn to fly, that they may be able to soar up with her towards the sun. So she hovers over them and tries to persuade them to stretch their wings; but the nest is far too cosy and snug for them to want to leave it, and they nestle down again in the moss and hay. But the mother knows all they will lose if they do not learn to fly, so she rakes out the wool and feathers with her strong beak, and makes the thorns and briars come to the top. Then, when all the soft lining is gone, the young birds shuffle about uncomfortably. The nest is not such a nice place after all, and by degrees they creep to the edge of it and sit there very miserably. And now the mother-bird again tries to get them to fly, and they spread their small wings, and she puts her great strong wing underneath them, so that they may not fall, and soon they are soaring with her into the glory above."

"Yes, go on," said Lady Violet.

"Do you remember that God says He is like that eagle? And so He rakes up the comfortable home nest, and lets us feel the prickles of pain and sorrow, not because He is cruel, not because He wants to punish us, but because He wants us to rise to something brighter and better, to the City of Sunshine. Now, Lady Violet, I'm afraid I've been preaching quite a sermon, and it is very good of you to listen; but don't you think this illness is one of the sharp thorns in the nest, to bring you to the edge, and make you care for something better?"

"Perhaps. I don't know, I'm sure."

They were silent for some time after this, and then Lady Violet said suddenly—

"It seems a pity now that I was ever engaged."

"Why?"

"Oh, it's such a nuisance for him, you see."

"Do you mean for the gentleman you are going to marry?"

"Yes. You see, he wanted me to marry him a long time ago, but I refused him; at least, I didn't actually refuse him, but there were reasons why I couldn't marry him then, one reason especially. But all that is over now, and I had just accepted him, and all was nicely settled, when this happened."

"But the doctor hopes you will be all right soon; doesn't he?"

"Oh yes, in time. But it's an awful nuisance for him having to wait; he wants to get settled. You see, he has only just come into his property; it's a nice little place, and he has a fair amount of money. It belonged to his mother's father; but some day he will come into a much grander estate, and be awfully rich. His brother owns it now, but he is getting an old man, and has no children. It's really a very good match for me, but it's a long time to wait, and I think he's getting rather impatient, and I did so want to have next season in town."

"Has he been to see you?"

"Oh yes, once or twice. Just before you came, he was here; but he lives a long way off, and I don't really want him to come too often — it's so tiring seeing people when you're ill."

Marjorie rather wondered at this remark. Surely if Lady Violet were very fond of her fiancé, she would not find his company tiring, although she was ill. However, she made no remark, but went on quietly with her work.

"Marjorie," said Lady Violet, presently, "you've never seen my photographs. I have two large albums full. Would you like to look at them?"

"Very much indeed. May I get them?"

"Yes, do. They're on the bottom shelf of that bookcase in the corner. Switch on more light, and sit in that armchair; you will see them better there."

Marjorie brought the albums, and sat down to look through the hundreds of photos with which they were filled — views of the park and the woods, of the church and the village, groups of various friends who had stayed at the Castle, photos of Lady Violet's horse and of the two St. Bernard dogs, river scenes and lake scenes, photos taken at all seasons of the year, some with the trees in full leaf, others with bare and naked branches, some showing the broad shadows of a hot summer's day, others taken in snow, with every tree and shrub looking as if it were growing in fairyland.

"They are lovely, Lady Violet," she said, as she laid down the first volume, and took up the one lying on the table.

SHE GAZED A LONG TIME AT THIS PICTURE.

SHE GAZED A LONG TIME AT THIS PICTURE.

"Oh! Those are foreign views. I don't know whether you will care for them so much. They are in the Riviera chiefly. We were there for a month about two years ago, and had an awfully jolly time."

Marjorie was turning over the leaves of the album, and had just been admiring a beautiful view of Monaco, when she suddenly came to one which brought all the blood rushing into her face. It was a photo of Lady

Violet sitting on a rock near the sea, and close by her side and looking over the same book with her was Captain Fortescue.

Marjorie would have known him anywhere; but she had never seen him look quite as he looked then. There was not a vestige of care on his face; he was evidently enjoying life to the full. She gazed a long time at this picture, and Lady Violet, glancing round, noticed how she coloured when she looked at it, and then how all the colour faded out of her face.

"Oh! That is a very great friend of mine," she said. "He helped me to take nearly all those Riviera photos. Evelyn took several of us together, and they came out very well. What is the matter, Marjorie?"

"Oh! Nothing; only it reminded me of some one I know."

"Did it? Isn't it awfully funny how one sees likenesses sometimes! Turn over; there are some more of him in that book. Isn't he good-looking?"

Marjorie did not answer; her heart was beating too quickly.

So he knew Lady Violet—yes, and admired her too; she could see that by his face in several of the photos where they were taken together. And what a handsome pair they made! They were just suited to each other. And now he was a lord; she had no doubt of it from that letter she had read. Had he discovered his parentage? Had he, in those long months since she had heard of him, found his father, and claimed his fortune? Could it be that he was the one whom Lady Violet was about to marry, the one who had admired her long ago, but whom she had refused because of some reason which stood in the way? Could that reason have been the loss of his money, and his being compelled to leave the army?

If so, Marjorie could quite understand that now this difficulty was probably removed. If he had found his father, if he had inherited a title, if he was heir to a large property, then surely no objection to their engagement could be urged.

Now, of course, she could see the reason of his long silence. It was now the end of March, and she had never seen him or heard of him since that October night when he had brought her home from Birmingham. Why had she expected to see him or to hear from him? How blind and foolish she had been!

Lady Violet seemed impatient that she should close the book, and Marjorie put it back in its place on the shelf. She wanted to ask her if Captain Fortescue was the one to whom she was engaged, but she felt that she could not bring herself to do so. She was so strongly convinced in her own mind that she was right in her conclusion, that she felt as if she could not steady her voice sufficiently to frame the question. Not for worlds would she have Lady Violet know what she had felt when she saw that photograph. How silly she had been! How foolish it was to have dwelt on what was merely a passing feeling of gratitude for a little service which she had rendered him! No one should know; no one should ever guess what she had sometimes thought and hoped. Least of all should Lady Violet know or guess.

So Marjorie talked to her on all manner of subjects, and was apparently never in better spirits, until at last the long evening wore away, and alone in her own room she could sit by her fire, and gazing into its red blaze she could pull down stone after stone of her fragile castle in the air, and then, when it was all laid in ruins, could pray for contentment and for peace. Surely she ought to be glad to hope that his troubles were over. Surely she should rejoice, if the desire of his heart had been granted unto him.

CHAPTER XXI
LORD KENMORE

THE spring ran its course, and the beautiful days of early summer began, and Marjorie sometimes felt as if she had lived at Grantley Castle all her life. It was a most restful time for her after the hard work of the year before, and she felt that she had much for which to be thankful. Lady Violet was still obliged to lie still, although her health and spirits were daily returning, and she was far less easily tired than she had been when Marjorie first came.

The house was now full of company, and Lady Earlswood, whose time was much occupied, was the more gratified that Lady Violet was so charmed with her companion, and that the arrangement she had made had thus turned out so satisfactorily. She was always very gracious to Marjorie, and Lady Maude thanked her several times for cheering up "poor dear Vi," as she called her. Lady Maude was full of life and spirits, and was certainly not cut out for a sick room. Her energy knew no bounds; she delighted in golf, motoring, and bicycling, and though she was fond of her sister and very sorry for her, she was of too restless a nature to stay long in the sick room, and was therefore very glad to feel that Marjorie's presence there enabled her to go to her various amusements with a clear conscience.

"Vi likes Miss Douglas," Lady Maude would say to her friends, "they get on wonderfully well together, and she keeps her in a far better temper than I can do."

So Marjorie had very few difficulties to contend with in her new position; even Collins the maid was glad that she had come and was able to relieve her from constant attendance on her young mistress, and from the fretful fault-finding to which she had been obliged to submit before Miss Douglas arrived.

Marjorie was very thankful for all this, and for the letters from home, which were very cheering. Leila was becoming quite strong again, and the money Marjorie was earning, and which she had been able to send home at the end of her first three months at Grantley Castle, had enabled her mother to buy many much-needed things for the household, and had considerably relieved the strain consequent upon the loss of the insurance money.

Marjorie searched the home letters carefully for any mention of Captain Fortescue, as she still called him to herself, but there was no allusion whatever to him. They had evidently heard nothing of him or from him.

Lady Violet did not speak to her again about her fiancé. She knew that she often had letters from him, and she wrote to him in pencil from her couch, but this was in the afternoon after luncheon, when Marjorie had gone out for her daily walk and when Collins was in attendance, and the letter had been carried down to the post-bag before her return.

But one wet day in the beginning of June, when Collins was lying down in her room, with a swollen face, Lady Violet said—

"Marjorie, will you get me my writing-case? I want to write to Lord Kenmore."

That was his name, then—Lord Kenmore. She would have thought that the missing word in the letter was a longer word than that; but she remembered that old Mr. Fortescue's writing was most uncertain and irregular, and he would probably spread out this name more than the rest of his writing, in order to make it clearer and more distinct.

Lord Kenmore. Could she ever think of him by that name? It all seemed so strange, so difficult to understand! But why was she letting these thoughts come into her mind? She had resolved never to think of him in that way again, never to recall that walk from Deepfields to Daisy Bank, or the grasp of his hand when he had said good-bye to her. She had been a foolish girl in the past; she would be a wise one in the future.

Lady Violet Kenmore. What a pretty name it would be! "Thank you for all you have done for me to-day." Of course he was thinking of Lady Violet when he said those words. He knew that she had not been able to accept him because of the loss of his money; but all that time, he had loved her, even though it had appeared hopeless. But now that the letter was found, which might enable him to prove his noble birth, and to find the clue which might lead him to recover his rightful possessions, he would feel that Lady Violet might still be his.

No wonder, then, that he had said so earnestly, "Thank you for all you have done for me to-day." No wonder that he had pressed her hand in gratitude, when she had been the means of bringing him hope. She saw it all now, and she marvelled at her former folly.

But all that was over now, and she took the letter from Lady Violet, when it was finished—the letter to him,—and carried it down to the bag.

"LORD KENMORE,
"Rockcliffe Castle."

That, then, was his address. She saw that, but she saw no more. What right had she to look at the letter to see his address? She would put it in the letter-box at once. It was nothing to her where he lived.

It was about a week after this, that one morning, as Marjorie was going out, Lady Earlswood asked her to go into the village to take five shillings, which she had promised to an old man, living in a cottage near the church, and who had once been a gardener at the Castle. She called at the cottage, had a chat with old Hill, and then went through the lodge gates, and began to climb the long ascent to the Castle.

The beech trees looked very lovely that morning in their pale spring dress, the moss by the side of the road being covered by the pale brown covering of the buds, which had fallen off as the leaves opened. The colouring was perfect, and Marjorie was thoroughly enjoying her walk.

But suddenly, as she turned a corner of the long avenue, far ahead of her, about a hundred yards or more, she saw something which took all the brightness out of her face. She saw Captain Fortescue walking rapidly towards the Castle. Yes, she was sure it was he. She could not see his face of course, but he was the same height, he had the same figure and hair, and he walked in the same erect way. All the feelings which she had been repressing and keeping down for so long rushed back into her heart.

It was hard work to walk steadily on towards the house. She felt dizzy and faint for a few minutes, and turned off the road and sat down upon the gnarled roots of a giant beech tree. But she prayed for strength and courage, and soon walked on again to the Castle. The road was empty now; she could see the great pillars of the portico and the closed door between them; he had evidently gone inside.

Once a wild hope darted across her mind that after all she had jumped to a wrong conclusion. Perhaps Captain Fortescue and Lord Kenmore were after all not the same; and if so, could it be that he had found out where she was, and had come to see whether she was happy at Grantley Castle, just as once before he had come to Daisy Bank?

But this faint hope was dispelled as she went upstairs, for Collins met her as she was going to her room, and said—

"Miss Douglas, perhaps you had better not go to my lady just now. Lord Kenmore has come to see her unexpectedly. His motor broke down just outside the village, and he had to walk the last part of the way."

Marjorie went on into her room, determined to be very busy and to give herself no time to think. She hoped, fervently hoped, that she would not see him. Perhaps he would not be able to stay long, and he would probably go downstairs for luncheon, and then afterwards she would go out in the garden or take a long walk on the hills. Meanwhile she would tidy her drawers, change her dress, and write home.

Marjorie found, however, that the writing was an impossibility; her thoughts would wander to the next room. How well she could picture him sitting in her usual place by Lady Violet's couch! How good he would be to her; how much he would feel for her in her suffering! What a comfort his sympathy and tender care would be to her!

And so more than an hour went by, and then came the sound of a bell, the bell of Lady Violet's sitting-room. This bell rang upstairs in Collins' room, so that her mistress could summon her whenever she required her. She heard Collins come down and go into the next room, and soon afterwards there came a knock at her bedroom door.

"Come in, Collins."

"If you please, Miss Douglas, my lady would like you to go to her."

Marjorie's heart died within her. He was still there, and now she would have to meet him. She wondered whether he knew that she was at Grantley Castle, or would he be surprised to see her there? Probably Lady Violet had told him, and, hearing that he knew her, had sent for her to come and see him.

With a prayer in her heart for help, Marjorie crossed the landing and went into the next room.

"Marjorie," said Lady Violet, "come here; I want to introduce Lord Kenmore to you."

Fearfully, almost tremblingly, Marjorie went forward, but, to her utter astonishment, a perfect stranger stood before her. His face was as unlike that of Captain Fortescue as it was possible for two faces to be. The figure, the build, and the colour of the hair were exactly similar, so that Marjorie was not surprised that, as he walked before her in the drive, she had imagined that he was Captain Fortescue; but the features, the eyes, and, above all, the expression of his face, were totally different.

Lord Kenmore was an exceedingly plain man, with the palest of blue eyes, which seemed wholly devoid of expression, with thin lips, a pallid, unhealthy-looking face, and a most cynical and unpleasant expression. How could she think for a moment that this was Captain Fortescue? He bowed stiffly when Lady Violet introduced him to her companion, and sat down again in the low chair beside the couch.

"Marjorie, I have been telling Lord Kenmore about the kind of paper I print my photos on; he is a photographer too. Would you mind getting those books you looked through the other day?"

Marjorie brought the albums from their place on the shelf, and handed them to Lord Kenmore. She was going to leave the room when Lady Violet called her back.

"Don't run away, Marjorie. Lord Kenmore is going down to lunch in a few minutes, and I shall want you then."

So she took her work-bag from the table, and sat down in the window, busy with a table-centre which she was working for her mother. She felt as if a great weight had been lifted off her heart; she had never realized how crushing the weight had been, until she felt the relief she experienced now that it had gone. Captain Fortescue was not Lord Kenmore! It seemed too good to be true, and he had not been thinking of Lady Violet when he said good-bye to her at Daisy Bank.

Meanwhile Lord Kenmore was turning over the photos, commenting on them as he did so. He was opening the Riviera book now.

"These are pretty!" she heard him say.

"Yes; we had a lovely time there two years ago."

"Hullo! Who's this?"

He had come to the very photo which had made Marjorie's face flush as she looked at it.

"Oh, that's a friend of Evelyn; they were at Sandhurst together, and we met him out there."

"I can't think who he reminds me of," said Lord Kenmore; "he's like some one. Dear me, who is it?"

"That is just what Marjorie said when she looked at that photo," said Lady Violet, laughing; "he is just like some friend of hers; he seems to be like a good many people."

"What's his name?"

"Captain Fortescue; perhaps you knew him at Sandhurst."

"No, I was at Woolwich; I can't think whom he reminds me of."

"There's another of him on the next page."

"Yes," he said, turning over the leaves, "he seems to have been fond of being taken with you, Vi."

"Yes, you see we saw a good deal of him there. He is very good-looking, isn't he?"

"Well, yes, I suppose he is. I don't care for that kind of face, though; he looks like a fellow in a cheap music-hall."

Marjorie was not half satisfied with Lady Violet's answer.

"Oh no, he isn't like that at all."

"Why, there he is again! A conceited sort of fellow, I should think."

Was he jealous? Marjorie wondered.

"No, he wasn't at all conceited," Lady Violet replied. "You would have liked him, I'm sure."

"Have you seen him lately?"

"No, not for ages; he has lost all his money, poor fellow, and is as poor as a church mouse. I don't know what has become of him."

Lord Kenmore seemed relieved to hear this, and there followed a long discussion on the relative merits of Ziga and Paget printing-papers, which lasted until the gong summoned Lord Kenmore to the dining-room.

"Will you put these books by, Marjorie?" said Lady Violet. "It was too bad of him to run down poor Captain Fortescue."

Marjorie saw no more of Lord Kenmore, for he had gone when she returned from her afternoon walk. Lady Violet seemed tired and out of spirits, she thought; perhaps she had felt the parting with him, it was only natural that she should; and Marjorie devoted herself to her more than ever that evening, and was determined to do all that she could to cheer her. She had such a light heart herself that it was not a difficult task to be bright and cheerful.

CHAPTER XXII
MR. NORTHCOURT'S OPINION

WHEN Kenneth Fortescue had left Marjorie at the door of Colwyn House, he blamed himself very much that, for even a single moment, he had allowed his feelings to be seen by her. Perhaps she had not noticed; he hoped not. For what right had he, a practically homeless and penniless man, to allow any girl to see that he loved her, or to attempt, in however small a degree, to win her love in return? It was cruel, utterly heartless and unworthy of a man, he said to himself.

For what hope of future happiness could such love ever bring? As long as he was so heavily in debt to her mother (for he refused to allow that the letter she had found had in any way cancelled that obligation) every penny of his salary, beyond what he actually required for food and clothing and the other small necessaries of life, must be sent to Rosthwaite. He intended to send it in future at the end of each year, and as his salary was a fairly good one, he hoped to be able to remit a substantial sum the following Christmas. But four thousand pounds was a considerable amount to reach, and he realized that it would take years before he could return it all, if indeed his life were spared long enough for him to do so. Meanwhile the thought of a home of his own was one of the many things denied to him, one of the indulgences which he had told Mrs. Douglas that he should renounce.

Moreover, as he travelled back to Birmingham, whilst he could not help a feeling of satisfaction that his origin was not so humble as he had imagined, yet at the same time, he reflected that his own father, whether he were a lord or not, was by no means a father of whom he could be proud. His foster-father, poor common miner though he was, had shown far more feeling than his real father, and had behaved in a manner which was vastly superior to that of the heartless man who had deserted his own helpless child, and had left him to the care of complete strangers. Still, if only that word had not been blotted out of the letter, he might have been able to prove his claim on that father's consideration, and might have compelled him to reinstate him in the position which was his by birth.

As it was, he knew not what steps to take. He decided at length to go to Sheffield, that he might see Mr. Northcourt, his father's lawyer, and take his advice in the matter.

Accordingly, the following week, Captain Fortescue travelled northward, and reaching Sheffield went at once to Mr. Northcourt's office.

The lawyer was much interested in the information laid before him. He read and re-read the letter several times; he took a magnifying glass and tried to discover the word covered by the ink; but at last he was obliged to confess that it was hopeless to attempt to decipher it. He was, however, strongly of opinion that the missing word or words had undoubtedly been the correct name. Watson and Makepeace would not have made that name illegible, had they not known beyond all doubt that it was the name of his lost father. What use they had made of that knowledge Mr. Northcourt said it was impossible to tell.

Probably the story that Miss Douglas had heard from the old woman in the cottage at Daisy Bank, and which Captain Fortescue had just told him, was perfectly true. They had found this name mentioned in the letter as the possible name of Captain Fortescue's father; they had then sought out and discovered the man named, and, by threatening to disclose what they knew of his past history, they had extracted large sums of money from him, money which they were now spending abroad, or which, quite possibly, lay buried with them at the bottom of the Atlantic.

Mr. Northcourt asked Captain Fortescue to leave the letter in his charge, as it would prove most valuable evidence, should the case ever come to trial, and he promised meanwhile to make all inquiries that were possible. At the same time he was obliged to tell Captain Fortescue that he much feared that no solution of the mystery would be forthcoming; the two guilty persons had evidently made good their escape, and he was therefore sorry to say that, in his opinion, they had not yet found the clue which would lead them to the discovery of Captain Fortescue's family.

After his interview with the lawyer Kenneth came away feeling rather downcast and disappointed. He was walking towards the station, hoping to be in time to catch the Birmingham express, for he wanted to get back that night, as he had work that must be done the following day, when he heard a well-known voice behind him.

"Captain Fortescue, sir!"

He looked round, and saw old Elkington, panting with the exertion of hurrying after him.

"Excuse me, sir, for stopping you, but I was so pleased to see you again."

"How are you, Elkington?"

"Fairly well, sir; I'm living with my daughter now; I'm too old to take another situation. Have you found it, sir?"

"Found what, Elkington?"

"The letter you lost, sir."

"Yes, I found it three days ago; at least a friend of mine found it, in the cottage of an old woman not far from Birmingham."

"Then it wasn't Watson who took it, sir?"

"Yes, it was Watson; she and that bookseller between them. He was her half-brother, Elkington."

"Was he, indeed, sir? Well, I never knew that! I always suspected her, sir."

"I knew you did, Elkington."

"She didn't like you, sir; she thought you kept her in her place."

"She wanted it, Elkington."

"She did, sir; but she didn't like it for all that. It was a bit of revenge, I should say, sir."

"Partly, Elkington, perhaps; but she and her brother raised money on it, too."

He then told Elkington a little of what he had heard, in which the old man was deeply interested.

"Was the letter what you wanted, sir? I mean was it worth having?"

"To a certain extent, Elkington, but those two rogues had blotted out the most important word, lest I should ever see it."

"The rascals!" old Elkington exclaimed. "Well, well; I'm not surprised at anything that woman did."

The old man insisted on going with the Captain, as he called him, to the station, and stood respectfully on the platform with his hat in his hand as the train moved off.

Kenneth Fortescue did not see that he could do anything further in the matter at present, nor indeed had he either time or opportunity to make any other attempt to solve the mystery of his birth.

He was now at the head of a large and important branch of a great fire insurance company, and had much business to transact. How could he neglect his only means of livelihood, in order to attempt to investigate a matter which baffled the legal mind of so clever a man as Mr. Northcourt?

Therefore, as the months went by, and brought with them a continuous stream of business engagements that filled up the moments of a busy life, there was left little time for thought or for brooding over the past. It was only when he had returned to his dull little sitting-room, and was resting by the fire for a short time before beginning his evening's work, that his thoughts would wander, in spite of himself, to Daisy Bank.

One evening, his eye fell on the photograph of Honister Crag, which was hanging over his mantlepiece. He looked back upon that walk with such happy remembrance. How much he had enjoyed it, and how far away it seemed now! He seemed to have lived a lifetime since then. He wondered how Marjorie was getting on. Was the hard work telling upon her? Could she keep her bright cheery spirit after so long a time spent in such dreary surroundings? It was six months since he had seen her. Was it really only six months? It seemed much longer.

Surely there would be no harm in his running over to Daisy Bank for an hour, the next time that he had a spare afternoon. He would be careful—very careful. Not a word or a look should reveal his secret. He would simply see her and come away, content if she were happy, and thoroughly satisfied if he knew no trouble was hanging over her.

At last the spare afternoon came, and he felt a great throb of pleasurable excitement as he got out on the Deepfields platform. Perhaps he should meet her on the road; it was the time when she usually took her walk.

But no, she was not there to-day. He walked on over the pit mounds to Daisy Bank. How long the way seemed! He passed the old cottage where his lost letter had lain so long; it was shut up and deserted. He hurried on now. Colwyn House was only a little further down the lane; he would soon be there, and would see her again.

He was going up to the door when he drew back in dismay. The windows were covered with dirt; several of the panes were broken; the steps were a mass of mud; the small garden was overgrown with weeds; the house which Marjorie had brightened by her presence was left untenanted and utterly desolate.

He stood looking at it for some moments in Hopeless bewilderment. A lad, who had come from his work in the pit, was standing near, leaning against a broken-down wall.

"How long has this house been empty?" asked Captain Fortescue.

"Six months, or maybe more," said the boy. "Have they moved to another house here?"

"No; they're gone."

"Gone where?"

"I don't know. Right away somewhere; down South."

"Why did they go?"

"The master fell down dead; soon after New Year it were."

"Do you know if Miss Douglas went with them?"

"Who did you say?"

"Miss Douglas."

"Never heard of Miss Douglas. They've all gone, so I suppose she did."

That being all the information he could extract from the boy, Captain Fortescue returned to the station, feeling much depressed by the result of his expedition. What had become of Marjorie Douglas? Would he ever be able to discover? He thought once of writing to Rosthwaite to inquire, but on second thoughts, he dismissed the idea promptly. What right had he to make such an inquiry? None whatever; nor did he see any prospect that such a right would ever be his.

So he went back to his hard work and his lonely life as contentedly as he could, and tried to banish the restless thoughts that came to disturb his peace of mind. He determined to take day by day as each came, doing the day's duty, bearing the day's care, and not allowing himself to indulge in daydreams of the future, which were never likely to become more than dreams.

CHAPTER XXIII
A MOST CHARMING GIRL

WHEN the autumn came round again, it found little change in Kenneth Fortescue's life, save that he had risen very rapidly in the esteem and confidence of his employers, and had been entrusted with the supervision of their agents in a still larger district.

Nothing, however, took place of a personal interest until the fourteenth of October. It happened to be the anniversary of the day on which Marjorie had come to him the year before, and which would ever be a red-letter day in his life, when he was requested by the head office to travel northwards, that he might investigate the amount of damage caused by a great fire that had taken place in a nobleman's castle, which was very heavily insured in his company.

Eagleton Castle was a most ancient building, filled with countless heirlooms of olden times. The picture gallery was hung with paintings by the famous artists of many successive generations; the grand staircase was of carved oak; several of the palatial rooms were wainscoted; whilst the great fireplaces were surrounded by exquisite carvings, the work of some forgotten genius, long since dead, who had left behind him these beautiful trophies of his skill.

These old mansions are exceedingly picturesque, and lend themselves to the work of the artist and the photographer, providing them with subjects for some of their best and most taking pictures, but they are oftentimes extremely unsafe. The builders of olden time, in spite of the roaring fires which in those days blazed nightly on the hearth, built the wide chimneys with little regard to the necessity for care in the matter of fire.

An old beam, in the near neighbourhood of one of the chimneys in Eagleton Castle, had become ignited; the fire had smouldered on for hours, completely hidden from sight, and unperceived by the large household of the castle. But in the middle of the night, a gale arising and blowing down the wide chimney shaft, had caused the smouldering fire to burst into a blaze; the floor of an adjoining room had been caught by it, and when the Earl and his household were at length aroused the fire was becoming serious.

Fire engines were at once summoned by telephone, and were soon on the spot; the servants were soon hard at work clearing the rooms in the vicinity of the fire; the numerous guests, headed by the Earl himself, carried out armful after armful of valuable heirlooms and piled them on the lawn in front of the castle; the firemen worked on manfully, but several hours passed before the flames were extinguished.

The damage done to the building was great; several ancient rooms were destroyed; but the most serious loss, in the Earl's estimation, was that of many of the works of art in the picture gallery. Some of these were family portraits, dating back for many centuries, and the loss of which could never be replaced. No amount of money could bring the dead earls out of their graves to be painted afresh; no compensation from the insurance company could ever restore to the Earl of Derwentwater those much-prized and valuable mementos of his long line of ancestors.

Still, whatever compensation could be afforded, in addition to the cost of those articles which it was possible to replace, would have to be supplied by the company in which the Earl had insured for many years; and the head office, knowing the capability and thorough trustworthiness of Mr. Fortescue, had requested him to personally visit Eagleton Castle, that he might report to headquarters as to what would be the probable extent of their liability.

It was for the purpose of making these investigations, that Kenneth Fortescue stood on one of the platforms at New Street waiting for the northern express. As he was looking at the signals and watching the line, he suddenly felt a hand on his arm.

"Fortescue, you here! I'm delighted to see you again; I thought I could not be mistaken." It was Captain Berington.

Kenneth was pleased to receive so friendly a recognition from an old acquaintance, whom he had never met since the day he had left Grantley Castle, after telling them the story of his life, so far as that story was then known to him. He knew more about his early life now; but he was not at all anxious to let his former friends hear what had come to his knowledge, and moreover, he felt that he was in one sense worse off than he had been before. Then he had a name which he thought he could call his own; now he was nameless.

However, he was glad to see Captain Berington again; doubly glad that Captain Berington seemed pleased to see him.

"Here's the train, Fortescue; let's get a carriage to ourselves, and then we can talk."

"I've a third-class ticket, unfortunately."

"Never mind; we can settle up with the ticket-collector. Here's an empty compartment. Get in."

"Where are you going, Berington?"

"Home. I'm awfully glad I met you. Now tell me all about yourself."

Captain Fortescue told him what he was doing, and mentioned that he was on his way to Eagleton Castle.

"What a terrible fire that was!" said Captain Berington. "It does seem an awful shame when old places like that are burnt. Vi was very worried over it. You see, Lord Derwentwater is Kenmore's half-brother, and Kenmore is heir to Eagleton."

"Who is Kenmore?"

"Oh! Don't you know? Vi is engaged to him. In fact, they were to have been married last year if it hadn't been for that nasty accident of hers."

"What was that?"

"Oh! Haven't you heard? She was thrown from her horse in the hunting-field. Came down on her back, poor girl. It was an awful thing. We were afraid she would not get over it at first, and then, when she seemed to have taken a turn, the doctors discovered that the spine was injured, and said she would have to lie on her back for months. It's been a terrible time for her."

"It must, indeed. How long is it since her accident?"

"Oh, nine months or more. She is a great deal better now. She gets out on the terrace, and is beginning to walk a little. They talk of having the wedding next May if she is well enough, so that it will just have been postponed a year. Poor girl, it has been awfully hard lines for her; but the doctor hopes she may be quite strong by that time. By-the-by, I've got a photo of her lying on the couch on the terrace. I'm just taking her a print of it; she hasn't seen one yet. I was at home a fortnight ago, and took it then."

"Then you are still keen on photography?"

"Yes, and I think this is a very good one. It was a nice clear September day, and I got a capital negative."

He was hunting amongst some papers in his pocket-book as he said this, and at last found the photo in question, and handed it to his friend for inspection. Captain Fortescue could not refrain from an exclamation of surprise as he looked at it. "You are astonished to see her so altered," said Captain Berington. "Yes, she is thinner, much thinner; still, she's wonderfully better than she was."

But it was not Lady Violet's altered appearance which had caused Captain Fortescue's exclamation of astonishment. He was not even looking at her; he was gazing with the greatest attention at something else in the picture. For on a low chair by the side of Lady Violet's couch, with her hat lying on the grass beside her, and with her lap covered with roses, which she was arranging in a china bowl standing on a garden table near her, was Marjorie Douglas!

He could hardly believe his eyes. For a whole year he had heard nothing of her; he seemed to have completely lost sight of her; and now at last he had found her, and in that unexpected place.

Captain Berington saw how earnestly Fortescue looked at the photograph; he thought that he noticed something more than mere attention in his gaze. Our eyes cannot always keep our secrets so well as our lips do, and there was a look in Kenneth Fortescue's eyes which told his friend a story about which his lips were sealed. But he interpreted that look wrongly.

"Poor Fortescue! I remember he was rather smitten with Vi once upon a time," he said to himself. "I ought not to have shown him that photo."

He put out his hand for it, that he might replace it in his pocket-book; but at first Kenneth did not seem to see.

"It's a beautiful photo, Berington! I suppose you haven't one to spare."

"Well, I am afraid not. I have another here, but I promised it to Miss Douglas; she wants to send it to her mother."

"Is she—"

Kenneth paused. He was going to say, "Is she well?" But that might have let out that secret of his, which his lips must guard with care. Captain Berington noticed his hesitation, but put it down to quite a different cause.

"She's an awfully jolly girl; she's a kind of companion to Violet—quite a lady though! It has made all the difference in the world to Vi having her."

Kenneth did not answer. He handed the photo back, though he would much have liked to have slipped it into his pocket.

"You've no idea what a nice girl Miss Douglas is! She is always good-tempered and cheerful, and never gets put out when poor Vi is cross. I'm sure we were awfully lucky to get her. She really is a most charming girl."

Kenneth Fortescue did not speak; perhaps because the words had moved him too deeply. And when, soon after this, his friend left the train, and he saw the carriage and pair waiting to convey him to Grantley Castle, a great feeling of loneliness crept over him as he leant back in the corner of the carriage.

Captain Berington was going to see her, to talk to her, and to give her the photo. And he thought her a most charming girl.

Kenneth wondered what Marjorie thought of him. Well, he must be glad that she was in a comfortable home, and was no longer toiling away amongst the pit mounds and coal dust of Daisy Bank.

CHAPTER XXIV
THE PICTURE GALLERY

WHEN, some hours after his parting with Captain Berington, Kenneth Fortescue arrived at his destination, North Eaton Station, he got out of the train with rather a heavy heart, and made inquiry of the stationmaster as to the best way to Eagleton Castle. He found there was a 'bus running from thence to the village, which was three miles away, and that this 'bus would start in five minutes. When he went out of the station he saw it at a little distance along the road, waiting for passengers. He jumped up beside the driver, and soon the jolting vehicle was carrying him towards Lord Derwentwater's beautiful old mansion.

North-country men have always plenty to say, provided that they do not live too far North and across the Border. There, the Scotch caution causes the words of the Lowlanders to be few, and their opinion on any subject hard to obtain. "I canna tell," or, "I wouldna like to say," will be all the reply you will obtain to your inquiry upon any subject. But with the North-country Englishman, it is different; out of the abundance of his heart his mouth speaketh, and he loves nothing better than to tell you what he has seen or heard.

The fire at Eagleton Castle, although it had taken place some days before, was still the great topic of conversation on the village 'bus; and, finding that Captain Fortescue was a stranger, the driver and the passengers united in giving him a detailed account of it, each being particular to relate how he or she had first heard of the fire, and how he or she had felt when the news was received. When these various versions had come to an end, Kenneth asked a few questions about the place to which he was going.

"Is it a large estate?"

"Tremendous; t' Earl, he is t' grandest man in all t' country round."

"Has he any family?"

"Neither chick nor child, and never had any."

"Who is heir to the property, then?"

"Lord Kenmore, brother to t' Earl. He don't come here much, though. Earl and him don't seem to hit it, somehow. They are only half-brothers, you see; t' old Earl was married twice, and the little 'un was born when his elder brother were growed up. Twenty-five years atween them. That was a lot, wasn't it? They didn't seem a bit like brothers; did they now?"

"No; it was a great difference in age," Kenneth said, "one brother was old enough to be the father of the other."

"You're right there, sir," said an old woman on the seat behind, "and the old Earl's second lady were a Tartar—a Tartar, that's what she were!" she repeated, nodding her head to give emphasis to her words.

"Ay," said the driver, "and she did her best to get t' old Earl to leave his money (what wasn't tied up of it, you understand) to the little 'un. She couldn't get him the title nor yet the estate, but she got him all that she could."

"Ay she did that," said an old man; "she were a crafty one, were my lady."

"But I suppose she had to leave the Castle when the Earl died."

"Ay," said the old man, with a chuckle, "and we none of us shed a tear; we didn't, I assure you."

"Then the present Earl came here?" asked Kenneth.

"Yes; he'd been travelling in foreign parts, but he came home afore t' old Earl died, and he married a lady o' these parts too."

"Is she living?"

"No, she lies in t' churchyard over there; ye can see t' old church tower over them trees."

"Has she been dead long?"

"It'll be about a year now. Since my lady died, he has had a good few of his friends at the Castle; there was some of them there for the shooting; t' Castle was pretty full t' night of t' fire."

"Was Lord Kenmore there?"

"Not he; he don't come here if t' Earl can help it. He's got an estate down South somewhere; he got it from his mother's father, so I'm told. We don't want him here; do we, Betty?"

"No, we don't," said Betty, "chip of t' old block, that's what he is."

"Does the Earl live alone?"

"Well, so to speak, he is alone. There's the visitors, of course; but they come and they go, none of them stay more than a day or two. It's a pity he hasn't got a son or a daughter to keep him company; isn't it now?"

"You like him?" asked Fortescue.

"Yes, we like t' Earl well enough; he's a bit hard sometimes, so folks say."

"But we're mighty sorry for him," said the old man; "he looks that wretched sometimes, my Tom says. Tom is footman up t' Castle. Now, sir, you look ahead and you'll see t' Castle up on t' hill."

Captain Fortescue looked, and he saw before him the most beautiful old castle he had ever beheld. It was built of grey stone, which bore the marks of age, though not of decay. Its mullioned windows had looked out for centuries over the beautifully wooded park, for the Castle stood on such high ground that it commanded a view of all the surrounding country; and the trees in the avenue which led up to it were many of them even older than the Castle itself.

Through this avenue of quaint oak trees Captain Fortescue walked, when he had left the 'bus at the great entrance gates. He lost sight of the Castle as soon as he entered the avenue, but he gazed with the greatest admiration on the loveliness which met his eye at every turn. Now and again there was a break in the trees, and he looked down a peaceful glade where deer were feeding in the shade of the silver birch wood; or he stopped for a few moments to watch a busy little stream which ran by the side of the road, and then disappeared beneath a rustic bridge into the depths of the woodland beyond.

The trees were putting on their autumn garb; the squirrels were running up the trees, busy in secreting the nuts and corn for their winter store; rabbits were scampering across the road to their holes in the mossy bank; a cock pheasant in his plumage was strutting along the road before him; and the whole place was alive with birds, which were singing gaily in the oaks overhead.

Then, as he drew near the Castle, he came upon an extensive lake, dotted with islands and surrounded by a plantation of lovely shrubs and ornamental trees. On this lake the swans were swimming gracefully in the sunshine of that autumn afternoon; the fish were splashing in the water; a covey of wild ducks had taken wing and were flying over the avenue; a heron stood at the edge of the water and was hunting for frogs. There was life and movement everywhere.

He looked at the Castle, and he marvelled at its beauty. He had thought Grantley Castle a fine mansion, but that was far more modern, and would not bear comparison for a moment with the ancestral home of Lord Derwentwater.

When Kenneth Fortescue had rung the bell which hung in front of the carved stone portico the door of the Castle was opened by a footman, to whom he handed his card, which bore his name and the name of the insurance company of which he was the representative.

"The Earl is expecting me, I believe," he said.

He was shown into a room not far from the entrance hall, in which the Earl was accustomed to transact his business. Here he found a gentleman of about his own age, sitting at a writing-table, and hard at work, with a voluminous correspondence spread out before him. He bowed as Fortescue entered, asked him to be seated, and told him that Mr. Montague Jones would arrive shortly.

"This is Lord Derwentwater's secretary, I suppose," said Fortescue to himself, as he watched his companion sorting and filing the letters with which the writing-table was covered. "But who in the world can Mr. Montague Jones be?"

After he had waited about a quarter of an hour, a stout man, with reddish hair, a florid complexion, and gold eye-glasses, made his appearance, and introduced himself as Mr. Montague Jones. He informed Kenneth that he was my lord's agent, and that my lord had requested him to conduct Mr. Fortescue, as the representative of the insurance company, to the scene of the late fire.

Leaving the secretary to continue his labours, Kenneth followed Mr. Montague Jones, as he led the way up a wide flight of stairs to the upper floor of the Castle. So far he had seen no sign of the destruction wrought by the fire; but, as they went down a long corridor towards the west wing of the building, they came upon the room where the conflagration had begun. Everything was blackened by the smoke and drenched with water; the furniture was either destroyed or completely ruined; the handsome silk hangings of the windows were gone; and a horrible smell of burning and charred wood filled the whole place.

From thence they went into the other rooms in which the fire had raged, and as they entered each Mr. Montague Jones handed him an inventory of the valuable articles which that room had contained; the pictures, china, statuary, pier-glasses, and costly furniture with which it had been filled; the carpet, curtains and elaborate draperies which had covered and adorned it.

These rooms were totally wrecked; the flames had spared nothing; the ruin was terrible and complete.

Then the agent led him on to the picture gallery, a long and wide corridor, having windows overlooking the lake in front of the Castle, through which the light fell upon the beautiful works of art which the gallery contained. The fire, however, had only reached one end of this corridor; some of the pictures were altogether unharmed, whilst others were merely discoloured by the smoke; but at that end of the gallery which lay nearest to the rooms in which the fire had broken out several large pictures had been totally destroyed, and many others had been hopelessly damaged.

"Portraits, all of them," said Mr. Montague Jones; "of priceless value to the Earl; family portraits that cannot be replaced. This one of the Earl himself, painted when he was a young man, has only just escaped."

What was it made Kenneth Fortescue start, as he looked up at that picture? What was it that made him deaf to the agent's voice, as he dilated on the Earl's loss?

The picture was that of a man of his own age, and the hair was his hair; the eyes were his eyes; the carriage of the head was his; the nose, the lips, the chin were the very counterpart of those which he had seen in the looking-glass that morning.

The portrait might have been his own portrait, painted yesterday.

What did it all mean? Was it just a chance coincidence? Or was it more? Was it the echo of the words he had read in that letter just a year before—"Mark this, Ken, you're as like your father as two peas are like?"

He wondered whether Mr. Montague Jones noticed the strange resemblance. No, he was a short-sighted man, and he noticed nothing. He was busily engaged with his papers, and with the notes he was making in his pocket-book for the benefit of the Earl. He saw nothing, he remarked nothing. He led Fortescue on to another picture, one much damaged, and which was hanging in a bad light between the windows. Kenneth looked at it absently. He spoke about it, but spoke as if he were in a dream.

As they passed that other picture on their way back through the corridor, Kenneth stood and gazed at it again. The likeness seemed to him more striking than before.

"There is no need to look at that one," said the agent; "it isn't damaged at all."

They left the picture gallery, and went down the wide staircase. Kenneth had no excuse for remaining longer. He had obtained the information which he needed for the head office; he would be able to write to London, giving a full account of what he had seen. Why, then, should he linger? What reason could he give for doing so?

The agent was walking with him to the door, when the busy secretary came out of his den.

"Mr. Jones," he said, "the Earl would like to speak to Mr. Fortescue."

Kenneth Fortescue was not naturally a nervous man, and he was not oppressed by the grandeur of the place in which he found himself. He had moved in good society, and he was able to hold his own in whatever company he found himself. The presence of an earl was no more embarrassing to him than the presence of that earl's footman. But if ever a man showed signs of nervousness—if ever a man hung back on the threshold of a room, as if he dare not face the revelation that the next step might bring, that man was Kenneth Fortescue.

But Mr. Montague Jones had preceded him, and he heard himself announced.

"Mr. Fortescue from the Insurance Office is here, my lord."

"Come in, Mr. Fortescue. I want to hear the result of your investigation. I want to know—"

What did Lord Derwentwater want to know? He seemed to have forgotten. He was looking at the representative of the insurance company with a strangely puzzled gaze. Only for a moment, though. In the next, he recovered himself, and began to give an account of the recent fire, and of the damage done by it, and his reasons for demanding so large compensation from the company.

Kenneth Fortescue looked intently at the Earl as he spoke. He wondered, as he did so, if he was looking at his own likeness, not of to-day, but of a quarter of a century hence. The features bore the strongest resemblance, but the hair was white, and the figure far less upright.

As the Earl spoke on, standing with his back to the fireplace, Kenneth stood facing him, apparently listening to his words, and yet in reality hearing nothing of what he was saying. He was looking for something—looking intently and eagerly. Why did the Earl keep his hands behind him?

Why did he stand in that position all the time he spoke? How could Kenneth ever discover that which he so much wanted to know?

But at that moment there came bounding into the room a beautiful collie dog, white as snow and with long, silky hair. It ran to the Earl, and looked up into his face. It was his favourite dog, his constant companion. He stooped to pat it as he spoke, and, as Kenneth looked at the hand laid on the head of the collie, he saw at last that for which he had been looking—he saw that the little finger of the Earl's right hand had lost the last joint.

Then, in a moment, he knew what was the missing word in the letter found in the safe; he knew beyond all doubt that he was at that moment standing in the presence of his own father.

CHAPTER XXV
WAITING FOR THE ANSWER

"WELL, I do not think we need detain Mr. Fortescue any longer. I want to speak to you for a few moments on another subject, Mr. Montague Jones."

It was the Earl who spoke, and his words roused Kenneth from a feeling almost of faintness which had crept over him, as he looked at the hand laid on the head of the collie. He bowed to the Earl, and at once took his departure. That was not the time to approach the subject on which his thoughts were centred. If he spoke to the Earl, he must speak to him alone, and not in the presence of Mr. Montague Jones; and, moreover, in his present tumult of feeling, he did not feel capable of speaking at all. He required time for thought and reflection.

He walked down the avenue, seeing and hearing nothing. The beautiful scenery was completely lost upon him. He passed through the great gates, hardly noticing the lodge-keeper, who opened them for him.

He went on, not knowing or caring where he was going, having not the least idea what course of action he should take. He wanted to be alone to think.

He found himself at last on a hill covered with Scotch fir trees. He climbed to the top of it, and sat down on a fallen tree. There lay the beautiful old Castle beneath him—his home—the home of which he had been cruelly deprived by the man he had just seen—a man who had no right to the name of father. A great feeling of anger rose up in his heart against this man, who was living in luxury and splendour, whilst his own son was struggling on, obliged to be content with the bare necessaries of life.

How could he ever pardon such heartless conduct? How could he ever forgive his father for his base desertion of him, when he was a helpless infant? His whole nature rose in revolt against such behaviour.

"'Forgive us our trespasses, as we forgive them that trespass against us.'"

Yes, he must forgive even this, if he would be the follower of Him who prayed for those who hung Him on the cross. He pleaded for help from above to enable him to do this, and as he prayed, he grew calmer.

Still he sat on, trying to plan what his next step should be. Should he go to Sheffield and see Mr. Northcourt? Or should he call at the Castle and ask for an interview with the Earl? Yet what if this interview was refused? What if the Earl had noticed the likeness, and, not wishing to own him, would henceforth be on his guard against seeing him again?

At length he determined not to go to the Castle, but to write. He would telegraph to the office that he was unavoidably detained at Eagleton; he would stay at the little village inn that night; he would despatch as soon as possible a letter to the Castle, and would await the Earl's reply. What would be the use of putting the matter in the hands of a lawyer, if his father were willing to own him? Why should their family affairs be brought under the notice of an outsider?

Kenneth returned to the village, sent off his telegram, and went to the Eagleton Arms. Then, after much thought and prayer, he wrote his letter.

He began by recalling to the Earl's memory events which had taken place twenty-five years ago. He reminded him of his early marriage to the girl he loved, of her death in the mining district in South Africa, and of the little boy she had left behind her. He asked him to think of the tiny deserted child, left in the custody of a common miner, with no evidence of his father's care save the money for his education. He then drew a sketch of the life of that child, at Eton and then at Sandhurst; brought up as far as his education was concerned in his proper position, but having as his only reputed relative the poor old miner, who had done all that in his ignorance was possible for him to do, to be a father to him. Then he described the death of that foster-father, and told of the letter that he had left in the safe.

Kenneth was careful to remind the Earl that the old man had faithfully kept the secret during his lifetime, according to his promise; but he told him that he had felt that, in making such a promise, he had done a great injury to the child left in his care; and that, therefore, he had written an account of what had happened in South Africa, and had left it with his will, to be opened and read after his death. Then Kenneth went on to tell the Earl that he was that deserted child, and to inform him that he had stood that day for the first time in his rightful home, and had beheld that day for the first time his own true father. He appealed to the Earl by all the love that he had had for his mother, by all the humanity of his heart, by all his sense of justice and right, to investigate the truth of his claim. He implored him to notice the remarkable resemblance between himself and the picture of the

Earl painted when he was a young man, and he entreated him to allow him to come to the Castle again, that they might talk together, and that the Earl might more closely observe that resemblance. He ended his letter by saying that he was anxiously awaiting his reply at the Eagleton Arms, where he should remain until that reply reached him.

It was late in the evening when the letter was finished, but he at once found a messenger and despatched him to the Castle. No sooner did he know that it was in the Earl's hands, than he began restlessly to await the answer. He felt as if he could not sit still a moment. He went outside and paced on the road; he reasoned with himself that no reply could possibly come that night; yet he still looked out for it.

But at length the Eagleton Arms was closing for the night, and he was obliged to give up his watch. He went to bed, but not to sleep. All night he was tossing about, wondering what the morrow would bring.

Then, with daybreak, he was up and out; he stood at the great gates, and looked at the morning light streaming down the avenue. What was that in the distance? Was it some one bringing the expected letter?

No, it was only a gamekeeper early at work, shooting the rabbits which were nibbling the short grass at the edge of the road. He went back to the inn and tried to eat some breakfast; but he felt as if he could not swallow it.

Then he watched again, and at last, at ten o'clock, a messenger came riding along the road from the Castle. He pulled up his horse at the Eagleton Arms.

Yes, he had brought a letter; the coronet was on the envelope.

The landlord was standing at the door. He took the letter and handed it to Kenneth.

"From the Earl," he said, "for you, sir."

Kenneth took the letter to his own room and opened it with trembling fingers. Then he read as follows:

"EAGLETON CASTLE,

"October 15.

"DEAR SIR,

"The Earl of Derwentwater requests me to state that he has no knowledge whatever of the subject matter of your letter. There will therefore be no necessity for you to call at the Castle. He regrets that you have been so grossly misinformed.

"Yours truly,
"HAROLD MILROY,
"Secretary."

Kenneth Fortescue felt as if he had received a heavy blow. What should be his next step? There seemed no object in remaining at Eagleton any longer. If the Earl flatly denied his claim, all that he could do would be to put the matter at once into Mr. Northcourt's hands.

Accordingly when he reached the railway station, he took a ticket for Sheffield, and arriving there some hours later, he was just in time to catch the old lawyer before he left the office for the night.

They were closeted together for a long time in Mr. Northcourt's private room, and Kenneth gave an account of his visit to the Castle. He told the lawyer of the picture he had seen in the corridor, of his interview with the Earl, and of the convincing proof which he had obtained during that interview, that the Earl was the man mentioned in old Mr. Fortescue's letter, inasmuch as he had noticed that the joint on his right hand was missing, just as Mr. Fortescue had seen and had described.

Then he told Mr. Northcourt how he had written to the Earl, and he showed him the downright denial which the Earl had given in the answer which he had received that morning.

Mr. Northcourt meditated for some time on the case of his client; but the longer he thought of it, the more his legal mind saw great difficulties in the way of substantiating his claim.

There were several questions which would immediately be raised by the other side; questions which, if unanswered, or if answered in an unsatisfactory manner, would most certainly render Mr. Fortescue's claim invalid. Who was his mother—Lord Derwentwater's first wife? They did not even know her name. Where were they married? They had no idea. Were they married at all? They had no proof whatever of the marriage, except the declaration of an old man who was now dead, and who had only stated it on hearsay.

If the marriage had taken place in the neighbourhood of Kimberley, search might have been made for the marriage register; but apparently, according to the letter found in the safe (to which Mr. Northcourt again referred, spreading it out on the table before him), the marriage, if marriage there had been, had taken place before reaching Africa in some place or other where his maternal grandfather had been chaplain; but what that place was, there was nothing in the letter to show, nor probably had old Mr. Fortescue ever known. Altogether it would be a most difficult case to bring forward, and undoubtedly further evidence would have to be obtained before the claim could be satisfactorily substantiated.

So Kenneth Fortescue returned to Birmingham, feeling as if he had been on the very threshold of Elysium, and then had been relentlessly drawn back into a land of toil, anxiety, and privation. It was hard to settle down again to the weary routine of his daily duties; the little back parlour had never seemed so dismal before. He was as far as ever from gaining his proper position in the world, and, whilst matters continued as they were, he saw no prospect of having a home of his own, and therefore no hope of being able to win Marjorie Douglas's love. And Captain Berington had every opportunity of seeing her, and he thought her a most charming girl.

Kenneth Fortescue was in very low spirits during those dark November days that followed. Heavy smoke-laden fogs rested on the city; the gloomy skies were not calculated to cheer him, and he had made no friends in Birmingham to whom he could turn to relieve the monotony of his life.

One Sunday evening he was walking through the muddy streets, which, with their closed shop windows, looked even more dismal than usual, when he heard the sound of a church bell. It was not the great church near his lodgings, and which he usually attended on Sunday. He had walked into a part of the city where he had not been before. It was a small church begrimed outside with smoke, and possessing no beauty within, a plain, unadorned building in a poor part of the city. He thought he would obey the call of the bell and go to the service. Perhaps there would be some word for him there that evening.

The clergyman was a tall thin man with stooping shoulders, not attractive in appearance, and his voice was certainly not melodious. But he had got his message straight from his Master, and Kenneth Fortescue had been sent to receive that message.

The words of the text fell upon his heart like the soothing touch of a cool, loving hand upon the fevered brow.

> "'O tarry thou the Lord's leisure: be strong, and He shall comfort thine heart; and put thou thy trust in the Lord.'"
> (Psalm xxvii. 14, Prayer-book version.)

Then came the simple sermon, devoid of all oratory, free from any attempt at grandiloquent language, as he urged his hearers to take the text as their watchword during the coming week. Each had his secret care; let him turn that care into earnest prayer. Then, having done that, let him wait patiently. God was sure to answer; but the answer must come in God's own time. Prayer cannot be lost; but we must not try to hasten God's hand;

we must tarry the Lord's leisure. Then, doing that, we shall be strong and comforted.

The preacher ended with a verse, of which each member of the congregation was given a copy on leaving the church. That verse was always kept by Kenneth Fortescue as one of his greatest treasures:—

> "Oh, tarry and be strong;
>   Tell God in prayer
> What is thy hidden grief,
>   Thy secret care.
> Yet, if no answer come,
>   Pray on and wait:
> God's time is always best;
>   Never too late."

CHAPTER XXVI
A CHRISTMAS JOURNEY

CHRISTMAS was now drawing near, and the Birmingham streets were as busy as on that day, two years before, when Captain Fortescue had seen Lady Violet at the door of the jeweller's shop in the Arcade. He wondered whether she was better, and if Marjorie Douglas had returned home.

He had saved fifty pounds during the year, and, two days before Christmas, he sent it to Mrs. Douglas with a short note, in which he said that he hoped they were well, and wished them all a very happy Christmas. He put another sentence in the letter, asking if Miss Douglas was at home for Christmas; but after he had written it, he thought it had better not be inserted. He tore the letter up, and wrote another.

On Christmas Day, an answer arrived. Mrs. Douglas thanked him very warmly for the money he had sent; it was far too much for him to have saved in so short a time. She feared that he was denying himself comforts which he ought to have, and had she not feared to grieve him by so doing, she should have returned the cheque. Not liking to do this, lest he should think her ungrateful, she could only urge him most earnestly not to attempt to send her so large a sum the following year. She was glad to tell him they were all at home, and quite well, and they united in wishing him every blessing and good wish for Christmas and the New Year.

Captain Fortescue was sitting in the old armchair by the fire in his room, reading this letter for about the tenth time, when Mrs. Hall came in to lay the table for dinner. She had insisted on his having "something decent to eat" (as she expressed it) on Christmas Day, and had cajoled him into the extravagance of allowing her to buy a chicken for his dinner. She had cooked it with great care, and now brought it in triumphantly and put it on the table.

"There's a beauty, sir, if ever there was one, and I've made some good bread sauce, and the greens are nice and fresh; I got them in the market yesterday, and there's some fine brown gravy."

"Thank you, Mrs. Hall; you take good care of me. I shall get spoilt if I stop here much longer!"

"Bless you no, sir! You'll never be spoilt, not, while my name's Mary Ann Hall—that you won't."

"Perhaps you are thinking of changing your name, Mrs. Hall?"

"Changing it! No, sir; catch me changing of it—not if I knows it. I've had one husband, and that's enough for me!"

Whether this was a compliment to the late Mr. Hall, Kenneth did not know. His landlady bustled out of the room, glad to think that her lodger would enjoy himself for once in his life. She had asked his permission to buy the chicken, but the plum pudding, which followed it, she had ventured to make without having received leave beforehand. He would only have said, "No, Mrs. Hall; I couldn't really eat anything more, even if you were to make it." Knowing that he would say this, Mrs. Hall had made her pudding without authority, and carried it in with great delight, a brown, well-boiled Christmas pudding, bristling with numberless almond spikes, like a porcupine covered with quills.

"There, sir!"

"Mrs. Hall! Mrs. Hall! What am I to do to you? You'll ruin me one of these days."

"Nonsense, sir. You'll never be ruined by a bit of Christmas pudding. Eat it while it's hot, sir. It's sickly-like when it's cold."

Kenneth had just finished this Christmas dinner, when there came a loud ring at the bell. Mrs. Hall went to the door, and presently returned with a yellow envelope in her hand.

"A telegram, sir! It went to the office, but the boy found it closed, and the caretaker sent him on here."

Kenneth took it from her, and opened it without any feeling of surprise or curiosity. Telegrams often came to the office, and he had left word that, in his absence, they were to be sent on to his lodgings. But when he saw the words on the pink paper inside, he started, and turned so pale that Mrs. Hall, who was waiting at the door to see if he wished to send an answer, could not help noticing it.

"Not bad news, I hope, sir?" she said.

"I hardly know, Mrs. Hall. Ask the boy for a form; I must send an answer."

It was a very short reply, soon written and quickly despatched—

"Coming immediately."

The telegram was addressed to, "Milroy, The Castle, Eagleton."

When the boy had been dismissed, Kenneth looked at the pink paper again. It simply contained these words—

"The Earl is ill—wishes to see you as soon as possible."

He got out his Bradshaw, and found that, being Christmas Day, there was only one train by which he could go, as the trains were running as on Sunday. There was no time to lose, for he must be in New Street in three quarters of an hour.

He made his preparations forthwith, hastily packing his hand-bag. He told Mrs. Hall that he had been summoned to a relative who was ill, and he managed to arrive on Platform 5 a few minutes before the train was due.

During the journey his thoughts were very busy. What would he find on his arrival? Had the Lord's leisure, for which he had been trying to wait patiently, at last arrived? He had trusted the matter to higher care than his own. Was that trust now to be rewarded?

It was late at night when he reached North Eaton. There was no 'bus to meet the train, and no cab could be obtained. However, after he had walked a little way along the dark road, he saw the lights of a carriage coming to meet him. It stopped when it came up to him, and the coachman, bending down to speak to him, said—

"Beg pardon, sir, but are you Mr. Fortescue?"

Kenneth having replied in the affirmative, he said:

"My lord gave orders that the carriage was to meet the last train. I'm sorry I'm late, sir."

Kenneth stepped into the carriage, and felt as if he were acting it all in a dream. He heard the gates opened by the lodge-keeper, then it grew darker as they drove beneath the overhanging branches of the oaks in the avenue. Now he knew that they were coming out into the open park; he could see the stars shining through the trees, and there was the moon rising behind the plantation on the other side of the lake. He knew that he was getting very near now, and his heart beat quickly at the thought. What reception would he have? What would he find when he entered the old Castle?

The carriage stopped before the great door; there was no need to ring. They were evidently expecting him, listening for the first sound of the carriage wheels, for the door was thrown open immediately. He was ushered into the library, the same magnificent room in which he had seen the Earl, the room in which the Earl's hand had rested on the head of the white collie.

The dog was there, lying before the fire. He got up and ran eagerly forward when the door was opened, but drew back disappointed when he saw a stranger enter, and threw himself despairingly on the tiger-skin rug.

In a few moments Mr. Milroy, the secretary, came in.

"I'm glad you've come, Mr. Fortescue; we have been longing for you to arrive."

"Would you mind telling me why you have sent for me? I have heard nothing as yet."

"The Earl is very ill, Mr. Fortescue, dangerously ill, I may say. We have two doctors in the house now; one or other has been here night and day the whole of the last week. To-night both are here."

"What is the matter with him?"

"It is the heart. I suppose he has had heart disease for a long time, so the doctors say, and every now and then he has a most alarming attack. He had an awful one the day after you were here last. We had to wire for Sir Lawrence Taylor at once, and he thought his condition then most critical. He fancied that the excitement caused by the fire had brought on the attack. However, they consider that he has been much worse this time."

"Does he want to see me?"

"Yes, indeed he does. In fact, he will give himself no rest at all until he has seen you."

"Do you know why?"

"I haven't the least idea. Perhaps you know, Mr. Fortescue."

"How should I know?"

"Did you not send the Earl a letter when you were here last? I remember writing an answer at his dictation. Now, whatever that letter of yours contained, I should imagine would be the reason of his wishing to see you now."

At this moment Sir Lawrence Taylor entered, and Mr. Milroy introduced Mr. Fortescue to him.

"The earl wishes to see you at once, Mr. Fortescue. It was quite against my judgment that he should see any one. Perfect quiet is essential for him, but I find that we shall have no hope of allaying the present alarming symptoms until he has had the interview upon which he insists. Will you, therefore, be so good as to follow me to his room?"

The doctor led the way, and Kenneth followed him.

They ascended the great staircase and went into a large bedroom, the mullioned windows of which looked out towards the front of the Castle. The bed was draped in costly Oriental silk hangings, and beneath these, and propped up by so many pillows that he was sitting more than lying, Kenneth saw the Earl. Two nurses were in attendance, and a doctor was sitting beside him with his finger on his pulse.

The Earl looked up eagerly as the door was opened, and Kenneth went forward and stood by the bed.

"My lord, you sent for me," he said, gently.

Lord Derwentwater motioned to Sir Lawrence Taylor to come near him. Then Kenneth heard him say in an agitated whisper—

"I must be alone with him. Tell them all to go out."

"My lord, you must promise me not to exert yourself more than is actually necessary."

"I will promise anything, only leave us alone."

At a word from Sir Lawrence Taylor, the nurses left the room at once, the two doctors followed them, and closed the door behind them.

As soon as they were gone, the Earl held out his arms to Kenneth, who was standing motionless by his bed.

"My son—my dear boy, come to me! Will you forgive me? Can you ever forgive me for the way in which I have treated you?"

Kenneth came close to his father, and the Earl put his arms round him and kissed him. He had refused to kiss him when he was about to forsake him, a poor, helpless, motherless babe; but now the kiss, so long withheld, was given, and the father's tears fell fast, as Kenneth knelt down by his bed and took hold of his hand.

"Will you forgive me? Can you ever forgive me?" the Earl repeated feebly.

"Freely—fully," said Kenneth, as he remembered the words with which he had that morning concluded his prayer, "'As we forgive them which trespass against us.'"

"I do not even know your name," said the Earl, piteously.

"Kenneth, my lord."

"Don't call me that," he said, impatiently. "I loved your mother, Kenneth."

"Tell me about her, father."

"Her name was Mirabel. She was the only one I ever really loved; her father's name was De Sainte Croix. He was of Huguenot descent, and was chaplain in Hyères when I was there. We were married at Hyères. Kenneth, I have written a statement, which will be quite sufficient, should I die, to put you in your right place. My lawyer was here yesterday. I made him read it through, and I signed it in his presence. The marriage certificate is with it, so there can be no difficulty about that."

"Thank you, father, for doing all this."

"Don't thank me," he said; "it's justice—common justice. It's what ought to have been done long ago. I can never make up to you for what is past. Who saw that letter, Kenneth?"

"What letter?"

"The one old Tomkins left in the safe. Some one must have got hold of that letter."

"How do you know that, father?"

"I know it because I have had threatening letters, anonymous ones at first, just vague hints of what might be done. But, after several of these had come, I had a mysterious visitor. He waylaid me one evening when I was walking in the shrubbery. I could not see his face well, he wore a long coat, and his collar was turned up, and feel sure that he was wearing a sham beard and moustache. He told me that he knew something in my past life, unknown to the world at large; he said that he had met a man whom he knew to be my son, born in South Africa, not far from Kimberley; and then he informed me that, if I did not give him a large sum of money, he would at once disclose my desertion of that son, and cause my secret to be known to the world.

"Kenneth, I never knew till then that you were alive. You were such a small, sickly child, that I had no thought or expectation of your living more than a few months at most. Then I did know, but not till then. The man waited for my answer, and I told him to come again to the same place at midnight. I went in to consider what I should do. The Countess was alive then, and I dare not let her know how I had deceived her. She would never have married me, had she known that I had a son; for her great desire had been to have a child to inherit my title and both our estates. But how could I, after all those years, let her know that I had deceived her? She was a hot-tempered woman, and there would have been an awful scene. So, like the coward that I was, I wrote the cheque, and gave it to him under the deep shadow of the great chestnut tree near the lake."

"Did you ever see him again, father?"

"Twice again, and each time he demanded a larger sum. At last I told him that I declined to give him another farthing, until he revealed the source of his information, and brought some proof of the truth of his statements; and from that day to this I have never seen or heard of him. Do you know who he is, Kenneth, and how he got to know?"

Kenneth gave his father the history of Watson, and of the disappearance of the letter from the safe, and then he told him what Marjorie had heard from the old woman in whose house at Daisy Bank the letter had been found.

"That explains it all, Kenneth. Now that brings us to the time of the fire and your visit to the Castle. When you came into the library that day, I saw the strong likeness to myself at once. I knew you must be my son. At one moment I thought I would send Montague Jones away, and would tell you the truth; at the next my heart failed me. What would the county families round think of my behaviour? What a revelation of cowardice and injustice it would be to the servants and tenants! How it would lower me in the estimation of every one I knew! Then your letter came, Kenneth, telling me facts which I knew to be true, leaving no room for speculation or doubt.

"You will wonder that my heart was not touched by it; I wonder at it myself. But I hardened my heart against you. I dared not lose the good opinion of my friends. Above all, I dared not tell Kenmore, my half-brother. He considers himself my heir; he prides himself upon it. I have been told that he has already planned how to alter and improve the park and gardens when I am gone. He does not care for me, nor I for him; but I felt that I could not bear the storm which this revelation would raise. But since then—that was in October, was it not?"

"Yes, father, the fourteenth of October."

"Since then I have been miserable, utterly wretched. I have felt sometimes as if Mirabel, my pretty little bride, came in my dreams to reproach me with the way I had treated her child. So I began to write the statement I have told you of; it is here, Kenneth, in this large envelope under my pillow. Take it, my boy; we will have no tampering with this letter. Keep it under lock and key, and never let it go out of your possession. I wrote it, Kenneth, and then I thought I would leave it with my lawyer, to be opened after my death. Cowardly again, wasn't it? But then this heart attack came on, and, Kenneth, something tells me that the next one will be my last. The doctors seem to be warding off the fatal consequences of this one, but another may seize me at any moment. And then, when I knew that, and began to face death, and thought of standing before my judge, my heart failed me. Of all the sins of my guilty life, I feel that this desertion of my own child has been the worst. And so I sent for you, and you say you forgive me."

"I do, father, indeed I do."

"Thank you, Kenneth; it's more than I deserve. I wish I could know that I had Divine forgiveness too, but I'm afraid that is out of the question now; it is too late for that."

"It is never too late, father; you forget how God longs and yearns to forgive us. He wants to forgive far more than we want to be forgiven. Why, He wants it so much that He sent His own Son to die for us, that He might be able to forgive us. You see He couldn't have forgiven us otherwise, for it wouldn't have been just. He is obliged to punish sin."

"Go on, Kenneth; I know it all in a way, but I want to see it clearly now."

"Well, you see, He let His Son be punished instead of us, so that when we come to Him He might be just, and yet able to forgive us. 'If we confess our sins, He is faithful and just to forgive us our sins, and to cleanse us from all un-righteousness.'"

It was the same verse which Marjorie had repeated to old Mrs. Hotchkiss, and the simple words, which comforted the heart of the poor ignorant old woman in Daisy Bank who could neither read nor write, now brought peace and a sense of pardon to the highly-cultured and refined nobleman. He grasped Kenneth's hand as he said—

"I will rest on those words, Kenneth, 'faithful and just.' Now I am afraid you must call the nurses. Get some dinner, and rest, and come to me again in the morning."

He grasped his hand warmly as he said goodnight, and Kenneth opened the door and admitted the doctor. He was leaving the room when his father called him back.

"Sir Lawrence Taylor, may I introduce my son to you—the future Earl?"

Sir Lawrence looked in astonishment at Kenneth, who was standing by the door; the nurses, who had followed the doctor into the room, also looked round in the utmost surprise.

"It is true, Sir Lawrence; this is my son. I have not seen him for twenty-five years, but before you all—" (he looked round at the nurses) "I own him as my lawful son and heir. I have sinned against him in the past, but from this day he shall take his proper and rightful place here. Good night, Kenneth; I must rest now."

Was the Earl wandering? Was the brain weakened as well as the heart? No, he was quite collected and calm. Moreover, they had only to glance at Kenneth standing by, with the signs of deep emotion on his face, and then to look from him to the Earl lying prostrate with exhaustion after the effort he had made; they had only to compare the two faces, to feel convinced that the words he had spoken were not the expression of some fancy of the wandering brain of delirium, but were, on the contrary, the sober words of truth and of justice.

A footman had been standing at the door with a tray in his hand, waiting to bring in beef-tea, which the nurses had ordered. He heard what was said by the Earl, and, needless to say, the news spread rapidly through the Castle. In the housekeeper's room, in the servants' hall, the strange tidings were eagerly discussed, and the stately butler, who came to the library soon afterwards, was the first to address Kenneth by the lawful title, of which he had been deprived during twenty-five years of his life.

"Dinner is served in the dining-room, my lord."

CHAPTER XXVII
ANOTHER CHAPTER CLOSED

SEVERAL months had gone by since that Christmas night on which Lord Derwentwater had acknowledged his son and heir, and Kenneth was now sitting once more in the little back parlour of Mrs. Hall's house, 156, Lime Street, Birmingham.

Those months had been most eventful ones, and he could hardly believe that the time he had been away had not been longer. Now, he had come to Birmingham to pack up his belongings, and to finally close his connection with the insurance company. He had been unable to leave Eagleton Castle before; his father had been loth to spare him even for a day. All the love which had been denied him for twenty-five years seemed to have accumulated, and was poured out upon him during the short time which they spent together. The Earl could hardly bear to lose sight of him even for an hour, and Kenneth devoted himself to his father, and was an unspeakable comfort and help to him in countless different ways.

Kenneth had the joy of knowing that the Earl was clinging with childlike faith to the Saviour of sinners, and that he was resting all his hopes on the finished work of Christ. He had passed away from earth, holding Kenneth's hand, only three weeks ago, and his very last words had been those which had first brought him comfort and peace: "'Faithful and just to forgive us our sins.'"

But Kenneth's first fortnight in the home of his ancestors had been an exceedingly stormy one. Lord Kenmore, on receipt of a letter from the Earl informing him of the existence of his son, had appeared on the scenes extremely indignant, and determined to vigorously contest Kenneth's claim. All his life he had believed himself to be the heir to the Derwentwater title and estates. His elder brother was married, certainly, but he had no family, and he therefore saw no prospect whatever of anything occurring to militate against his succession. He had told Lady Earlswood what his prospects were, and, on the strength of them, she had given her consent to her daughter's engagement. The estate which he had inherited through his mother was comparatively a small one, the rent-roll was a mere bagatelle, when compared with that of Eagleton.

And now, just when Lady Violet was recovering from her accident, when the date of their wedding was once more fixed, when all their arrangements were made, and when everything seemed going well, this letter from the Earl had arrived, informing him that a son of his, ignored and disowned for twenty-five years, had turned up, had been received and welcomed, and was now to inherit his title and estates.

The story appeared to Lord Kenmore to be simply incredible; he could not bring himself to believe that it was founded on fact; he would not, even for a moment, accept such a ridiculous statement, even though he had it in the Earl's own handwriting. His brother's repeated heart attacks, which rendered his life so uncertain, had made him, not unnaturally, calculate upon a speedy succession to the glories of Eagleton Castle. Was it likely then that he would meekly submit to being disinherited, or would allow without a hard struggle that those glories would never be his own?

Thus Lord Kenmore drove up to the Castle in a towering passion, marched past the footman and butler, walked imperiously upstairs, and demanded an interview with the Earl immediately.

When the doctors told him that this was impossible until the next day, as the Earl was extremely weak that evening and must be kept perfectly quiet, he was more angry still; and when he discovered, from the servants, that the impostor, as he called him, was at that very time sitting in the Earl's bedroom, to which he was admitted at all hours of the day and night, his indignation knew no bounds. He utterly declined to take the slightest notice of Kenneth or even to see him. He ordered dinner to be served in his own room, as he did not choose to sit down with the man who had supplanted him, and he went to bed that night determined to fight to the last for what he chose to call his lawful rights.

But the following day, Lord Kenmore was admitted to the Earl's presence, and going into the room he found the family lawyer sitting by the bedside. On a table before him lay the indisputable proofs of the marriage and of the child's birth, and bit by bit the lawyer, who was the spokesman on the occasion, showed Lord Kenmore that, if he attempted to establish his claim in a court of law, he would simply incur great and needless expense, for he would be perfectly certain to lose his case.

"I'm sorry, very sorry, Kenmore, that you have been kept in ignorance of this so long," said the Earl, "and I feel very much for you in your disappointment; but I must do justice to my own son."

Thus the interview ended, and Lord Kenmore, still only half convinced, ordered the carriage, and drove away from the Castle, without having even met the nephew who had taken his place.

He wrote many angry letters after his return home, but after taking further legal advice, he was at last compelled to own, sorely against his will, that nothing could be done to reverse the ill-luck which had fallen upon him.

There was great consternation at Grantley Castle when the news arrived there. Lady Earlswood felt that Lady Violet's prospects were now far below her expectations. Had she known that Lord Kenmore was a comparatively poor man, she would never have consented to the engagement. However, now it was too late to draw back, and she must hope to find a better settlement for her younger daughter. Perhaps this son of Lord Derwentwater might be eligible; he was a young man, and she gathered from Kenmore's letter that he was unmarried. She had no idea who he was. Lord Kenmore told her that he had been born in Africa, and that he thought he had turned up from some place abroad. Never for a moment did either she or her daughters connect him with the son of the rich miner whom they had discarded two years ago, and whom they now supposed to be earning his living somehow or other in a very humble manner. Captain Berington had not mentioned his meeting with Kenneth, and they had heard nothing of him since the day that he left Grantley Castle.

When, some time after, the news of the death of Earl Derwentwater reached her, Lady Earlswood at once determined to cultivate the new Earl's acquaintance. He must most certainly be invited to the wedding. He was Kenmore's nearest relative, and, although she knew that her future son-in-law was angry with him at present, he must be made to see the importance of a reconciliation with his brother before the grand event took place. Lady Maude was still an unappropriated blessing, and who could tell whether she might not have a chance of gaining the title which her sister had unfortunately lost?

During the latter part of the Earl's life, he and his son had been left in peaceful enjoyment of each other's society. He recovered from his severe illness to a great extent, and was able to be moved daily on to a couch in his own room; but on the fourteenth of March another heart attack had occurred, more violent than any of those which had preceded it, and in the space of a few hours he had passed away.

Lord Kenmore would not even come to his brother's funeral, and uncle and nephew had therefore never met.

Now Kenneth had at last been able to leave the Castle, and had come to Birmingham to wind up his affairs there, and was therefore sitting to write his letters in his old place in Mrs. Hall's dismal little room. She was very sorry to lose her lodger, and told him that she would never have another like him. He had paid her in full for all the time he had been away, and had delighted her heart by the present of a new carpet and some pretty furniture to adorn her little room.

"Well, now, to be sure, if ever there was a gentleman, he's one!" she would say to her friends.

Kenneth, as he sat at the table in the window, was writing a letter to Mrs. Douglas. If we had looked over his shoulder, we should have seen that it ran thus:

"156, Lime Street, Birmingham,

"April 3.

"DEAR MRS. DOUGLAS,

"I am hoping to have the pleasure of calling upon you some time next week. I was so charmed with the peep I had of Borrowdale two years ago, that I am planning a little holiday in your beautiful neighbourhood, and I think of making the comfortable inn at Rosthwaite my headquarters during the time I am in Cumberland.

"I am glad to be able to tell you that I am receiving more money this year, and therefore hope that my next remittance will be a somewhat larger one.

"With kind regards,

"Yours sincerely,

"KENNETH FORTESCUE."

He read this letter through several times after he had written it. He had purposely addressed it from his old lodging in Birmingham. He had carefully concealed his present position. Had she not said, "I rather hope you are not a lord; you would seem so much less our friend."

Why, then, should he tell her? He would go unattended, as the poor man he had been when she saw him last; then she would feel that no wide social gulf had come between them. He had no fear of her discovering otherwise who he was; even Kenmore would never connect him with the Captain Fortescue of whom he might possibly have heard at Grantley Castle. In the Earl's statement, his foster-father had been called by his proper name, Tomkins; the name Fortescue had not even been mentioned. So that Kenneth felt sure that his secret was safe, and he hoped that therefore he would not seem "so much less their friend."

He had to spend two days in Birmingham winding up his accounts, and at the end of them, he received Mrs. Douglas's answer. She told him that she was glad to get his letter, and that they would all be very pleased to see him again in Borrowdale.

Kenneth hoped from this letter that he might find them all at home. He had had a letter from Captain Berington at Christmas, in which he told him that Violet was quite well again, and that he was sorry to say that Miss Douglas was leaving. He wondered whether Marjorie had by this time undertaken any other work. He could not help hoping that she was included in the all in her mother's letter.

When at last his packing was finished, Mrs. Hall took an affectionate farewell of her lodger. He told her that he would like to hear now and again how she got on, and he would therefore give her his future address. He handed her his card, and when she had glanced at it she turned quite pale.

"Who's this, sir?" she said. "This isn't your name!"

"It is, Mrs. Hall—my very own."

"But you're not an earl, surely!"

"Yes, I am, Mrs. Hall."

"Deary me! And I've waited on you and scolded you when you wouldn't get better dinners. I'm fair scared, sir!"

Kenneth laughed at her dismay.

"Never mind, Mrs. Hall," he said, shaking hands with her at parting. "You've been a good friend to me, and I shall never forget your kindness."

"To think of that!" Mrs. Hall would say to her friends. "I've waited on a real live earl! I'm not half proud!"

CHAPTER XXVIII
WATENDLATH FORGET-ME-NOT

BORROWDALE is beautiful at every season of the year. The summer sunshine lights up its purple, heather-covered heights; the autumn tints make the wood in its hollows ablaze with orange and red; and the winter snows give it a grand and Alpine appearance.

But the hand of spring, after all, lavishes most loveliness upon Borrowdale. It covers it with a carpet of primroses, it draws through its woods a pale-blue lining of wild hyacinths, it makes its fields into cloth of gold with buttercups; whilst the fresh green of the silver birch, the bursting buds of the chestnuts, the countless signs in every flower, bush, and tree of awakening resurrection life, combine to make the whole valley a perfect fairyland.

So Marjorie Douglas thought, as she set out that spring morning, and began to climb the hill behind Fern Bank, in order that she might pay her weekly visit to one of her favourite old women. Her heart was as full of brightness as the spring day, for was not this the week in which Captain Fortescue had said he was coming to Rosthwaite? She had not seen him for a year and a half, and had heard nothing of him, save those two short notes which he had written to her mother. Evidently he had never yet discovered the missing word in the letter, for he was still living in Birmingham, in that dismal little house in Lime Street.

She was glad that he was going to have a little holiday from his hard work. She was pleased to think that Borrowdale would look its very loveliest when he arrived, and she knew that her mother would be glad to see him and to have a talk with him again.

As for herself—well, perhaps, she would be glad too.

The path led her through a copse wood where the primroses were a sight to see, and then, as she went higher still, she came upon a rough mountain road. She followed this for some way, and, after a stiff climb over the moorland, she came to the little hamlet of Watendlath, which nestles in a hollow amongst the hills. A more picturesque place could scarcely be found; the few white farmhouses and small thatched cottages stand by the side of a quiet mountain tarn, and are reflected in its still waters; the little village seems completely shut off from the world by the mountains which surround it.

Old Sarah Grisedale lived in a cottage at a little distance from the lake. She was a tall, thin old woman, active, in spite of her great age, and still able to walk over the mountain to church, and to climb the steep hill again without even the help of a stick.

Marjorie had a long chat with her old friend, sitting in her usual place on a three-legged wooden stool in front of the peat fire, and then she emptied her basket of the good things she had brought for her, and went on to an ancient farmhouse standing just above the tarn, that she might buy some eggs which her mother had asked her to get there. Several dogs ran out barking when she drew near; but they knew Marjorie well, and were quiet as soon as she spoke to them.

The old farmhouse has stood in this secluded spot for many hundreds of years, and its low ceilings, oak panelling, heavy wooden beams, deep chimney corners, and carved cupboards are all relics of the days of long ago.

When Marjorie left the farm, she crossed the little bridge over the stream running into the mountain tarn, and as she did so, she noticed that growing by the edge of the water was a quantity of large blue forget-me-not. She climbed down the bank to the water and gathered the blue flowers, and then sat down on the grass to pull off the wet roots which had come up as she plucked it, and to arrange the flowers in her basket above the eggs.

As she did so, sitting by the side of the rushing brook and hearing nothing but its noisy babbling, she was startled by feeling something bounce against her arm. It was a large white collie, which had come bounding down the steep bank, and which now lay down beside her, putting its paws on her knees.

"O you beauty, you lovely fellow!" said Marjorie, as she stroked the dog's head. "Where have you come from, and whose dog are you?"

She was not left long in doubt on this point, for the dog's master was close at hand. She heard a voice behind her, a voice she knew well.

"Miss Douglas, I've found you at last."

"Captain Fortescue! How did you know I was here?"

"I called at Fernbank, and Mrs. Douglas told me you had come up the hill, so Laddie and I came in search of you."

He climbed down the bank and took her hand in his.

A piece of forget-me-not fell at his feet as Marjorie got up to speak to him. He picked it up and asked, "Is it for me?"

"If you like," she said in a low voice.

"I expect you thought I had forgotten you," he said; "but there is no need to give me the little blue flower, I assure you, Miss Douglas. I have never forgotten you. I never could forget what you did for me the last time I saw you."

"And yet it was all of no use," she said sadly.

"Don't say that. Who can tell? That letter may yet prove to be a most important link in the chain. What a lovely place this is! Shall we sit here and talk a little? It is so quiet and beautiful."

They sat down on the rocky bank, and the collie laid his chin on Marjorie's arm and gazed up into her face.

"Tell me what you have been doing the last eighteen months, Miss Douglas."

She told him of Mr. Holtby's death, and how they had all left Daisy Bank.

"Yes," he said, "I went there one day to see you, and found you gone."

"Did you? I wish I had known!"

"Why? Oh, I see. You thought I had forgotten. Well, where did you go next?"

"I went to some friends of yours, very great friends, I believe. I was companion to Lady Violet Berington."

She glanced doubtfully at him as she said this, as though she wondered whether the mention of the name would give him pain, but she was reassured by his face. There was no trace of anything in it but great interest in her story.

"I wonder how you found out that I knew them."

"I saw your photograph in Lady Violet's book."

"Yes, in the Riviera. I remember I was taken with her a great many times."

"And I thought—"

"What did you think?"

"You will laugh when I tell you! I thought you were Lord Kenmore."

"Kenmore, of all people on earth! Why did you think that?"

"I knew that Lady Violet was engaged to Lord Kenmore, and I thought that perhaps Kenmore was the missing word which we tried to read in the letter."

"I see. And you thought Lady Violet and I seemed very much together in the photos? I understand now. Have you seen Lord Kenmore?"

"Yes, once; he came to see Lady Violet, and I went into the room expecting to see you. I had followed him up the avenue, and he looked exactly like you in the distance. Have you ever met him, Captain Fortescue?"

"Never."

"His figure is really very like yours, and his hair and the way he walks— really very much alike; but his face is quite different."

"Were you glad or sorry when you found that I was not Lord Kenmore?"

Marjorie did not answer, and he repeated the question; but she was busily throwing the forget-me-not flowers on the water, and watching them float under the bridge, and still she did not speak.

"How long were you at Grantley Castle, Miss Douglas?"

"I left at Christmas. Lady Violet was quite well then."

"Were you sorry to leave?"

"Yes, in some ways; it's a lovely place, and they were really very good to me, all of them. I think, I am sure Lady Violet would have liked me to stay a few months longer, to help her in the preparations for her wedding; but—"

"But what?"

"Well, I fancy Lady Earlswood was anxious that I should not stop longer. Captain Fortescue, do you know Captain Berington?"

"Yes, of course I do; we were at Sandhurst together."

Marjorie stopped, as if she did not like to say more.

"Please go on, Miss Douglas. What about Captain Berington?"

"Well," she said, "perhaps I ought not to say it, especially as you know him, but I rather think it was on his account that Lady Earlswood wanted me to leave."

"Why on his account?"

"Well, he was very kind to me, and when I went for my afternoon walk in the park, he often happened to be going in the same direction. I couldn't help it, could I? But I think Lady Earlswood thought I could; and it was rather uncomfortable, you see, so I was glad to get away."

"Really glad?"

"Yes, really glad. It was so very awkward. I did not want him to come, but he always seemed to turn up wherever I went, and I did not know what to do."

"So you came home at Christmas?"

"Yes, on Christmas Eve."

"Have you heard from any of them since?"

"Only once. I had a letter from Lady Violet a few weeks after I left, saying there was some disturbance about Lord Kenmore's property, or rather the property which he expected to get at his brother's death, and she was afraid he would be robbed of what rightfully belonged to him; but she did not say what the trouble was, nor who wanted to rob him. That was in January, and I have never heard since."

"Not from any of them?"

"Oh no. Now, will you tell me what you have been doing?"

"Well, things have brightened a bit for me. As I told Mrs. Douglas in my letter, I am better off than I was. I am leaving Mrs. Hall."

"Poor Mrs. Hall!"

"Yes, she seems sorry to lose me, good old soul!"

"Where are you going to live? At the other end of Birmingham?"

"No, quite out in the country."

"Not the Daisy Bank way?" she said, laughing.

"No, north of Birmingham."

"I'm so glad you will be in the country! I love the country, and it will be so restful for you after your hard work in the city."

"Yes, I hope it will; I feel sure it will."

"What is the name of the place?"

"North Eaton."

"Have you got nice lodgings there?"

"No, I am not going into lodgings again. I am going to start housekeeping."

"Housekeeping! Have you got a house?"

"Yes, I have got a house. I have had one for a few weeks now."

"Is there a garden?"

"A very nice garden; and the house is—well, rather a nice house, I think. It only wants one thing. Marjorie dear, can you not guess what that one thing is?"

She was bending over Laddie, so that he could not see her face.

"Can you guess, Marjorie?"

She shook her head.

"You can't guess?" he whispered, as he took hold of the hand which was stroking Laddie's head. "Then I shall be obliged to tell you; Marjorie darling, it wants you!"

CHAPTER XXIX
THE MISSING WORD FOUND

IT was a lovely morning in June, and the little village of Rosthwaite was all astir, and filled with pleasurable excitement. Some were standing at their doors; others were looking out of their windows; from many a farm on the hillside, from many a lonely cottage, people were coming in little groups towards the church; the whole place, so quiet at other times, was filled with life and movement. Work was laid aside, every one was in holiday attire, for it was Marjorie Douglas's wedding-day.

Every one loved her; she had grown-up amongst them from childhood; she had gone in and out amongst them as a friend, and they were loth to part with her. But on her wedding-day, they must not think of that; she must see none but bright faces. Old Mary had hobbled on her stick all the way from Seatoller; Sarah Grisedale had come down from the mountains, and had waited an hour in the churchyard before the time of the wedding; and many another whom Marjorie had cheered and comforted was to be found in the little church, to pray for a blessing on the fair young bride.

The wedding was by licence; and the Vicar, at the bridegroom's dictation, had filled up the required information in the register before the arrival of the bridal party. Only two people knew what name was written there, above the name of Marjorie Douglas. The clergyman knew, of course, for he had written the words; and Mrs. Douglas knew. Kenneth had told her the night before. Marjorie herself had no idea, as yet, of the future that lay before her, or of the name which would that day become hers.

It was a very pretty though quiet wedding; and as Mrs. Douglas heard Kenneth's manly voice saying, in tones of deepest feeling:

"I, Kenneth, take thee, Marjorie, to my wedded wife," she felt that she was giving her child to one whom she could fully trust, one who was not only a kind and honourable man, but who was, above all things, a true servant of the Lord Jesus Christ.

Then came the signing of the names in the marriage registers. Mrs. Douglas was talking to Marjorie whilst Kenneth signed both books, and then the clergyman called her to write her name below. He had placed the blotting-paper over the upper line on which Kenneth's name stood.

"Do you mind leaving it there, Marjorie?" he said. "I am very particular about the neatness of my registers, and the lace on your sleeve may blot it."

Marjorie laughed, and wrote her name without removing the blotting-paper which covered the entry above. Then the books were closed, and the bridal party drove to Fernbank, amidst the cheers and good wishes of the villagers.

About an hour afterwards, Colonel Verner's carriage stood at the gate, waiting to convey the bride and bridegroom to Keswick station, and Kenneth and Marjorie came down the pretty garden, followed by the whole family, including good old Dorcas. Then the last good-byes were said, and they drove off; but at the bridge Kenneth stopped the carriage; he had forgotten his stick, he said.

He soon returned with it; but Marjorie did not know that he had purposely left it behind, in order that he might be able to slip a small envelope into her mother's hand. And when Mrs. Douglas opened it, after the carriage had driven away, she found that it contained a cheque for four thousand pounds.

The honeymoon was not to be a long one; only a fortnight in Scotland amidst the beauties of the Northern Highlands. Kenneth was anxious to get back to Eagleton, for he had much to arrange there, and Marjorie was eager to see her new home.

She asked many questions about it during their wedding tour.

For example: "Would all be ready when they arrived?"

"Oh yes; the servants were there."

"Servants! Would they be able to afford to keep two? Would it not be too extravagant?"

He could not help smiling when she said this, and had nearly let his secret out.

"Wait till you get home, Marjorie," he said, "and if you then think it is too many, we can send one away."

At another time she wanted to know how many rooms there were in the house, and what it was like. He told her that he was a bad hand at describing places; she would see when she got there.

"Is it a large house?"

"Larger than Mrs. Hall's."

"As big as Fernbank?"

"Yes, he thought it was quite as big as Fernbank."

And so the happy fortnight passed away, and the day arrived on which they were to return home.

"First-class tickets again. How extravagant you are, Kenneth!" she said, as they got into the train.

"One isn't married every day, Marjorie, and this is our honeymoon, remember."

"We are getting near North Eaton, Marjorie," said Kenneth, some hours after. "I think it is the next station."

Marjorie looked eagerly out of the window. "What lovely country!" she said. "I am so glad it is such a pretty place."

"The train is slowing down now, Marjorie."

"Oh, Kenneth, there is such a beautiful carriage waiting at the station, with a pair of lovely cream-coloured horses!"

"Very likely. There are several large estates in the neighbourhood."

A footman was standing on the platform, and came to the carriage door touching his hat. Kenneth got out and spoke to him, and walked with him a little way down the platform. Then he came back to where Marjorie was standing.

"Now, Marjorie, we will go to the carriage. Charles will see after the luggage."

"What carriage?"

"The one you saw standing on the road outside."

"Whose is it?"

"Lord Derwentwater's; it is going to drive us home."

"Do you know Lord Derwentwater, Kenneth?"

"Yes, very well."

"How very kind of him to send his carriage for us! Isn't it, Kenneth?"

They got in, and were soon driving rapidly along the road to Eagleton.

"Shall we soon be home?" she asked presently.

"Yes, very soon now. It is about two miles, I think."

Marjorie was too excited even to talk now. She was longing to see her new home, of which she knew so little.

"Kenneth," she said, about ten minutes later, "where are we going? They are stopping before a lodge, and they are opening the great gates. They must have made some mistake."

"No mistake at all, dearest; it is quite right."

"But look at this lovely avenue! We seem to be getting near some very grand house. Are you sure it is all right, Kenneth?"

"Quite right, darling. Look out; you will see the house in a few minutes."

They came out of the shade of the avenue into the bright evening sunshine beyond, and there before them, in all its magnificence, stood Eagleton Castle.

"Marjorie, do you like your home?"

"Kenneth," she said, in a half-frightened whisper, "I can't understand it. What does it all mean?"

"It means, my dear little woman, that I have found out the missing word in the letter, and that you are Lady Derwentwater."